Catalina and the Winter Texan

by

Hebby Roman

Hebby Roman

Copyright

This is a work of fiction. Names, characters, places, and incidents are either the product of the author's imagination or are used fictitiously, and any resemblance to actual persons living or dead, is business establishments, events, or locales, is entirely coincidental.

Catalina and the Winter Texan
COPYRIGHT © 2015 by Hebby Roman
Published by Estrella Publishing Inc.
Cover designed by Earthly Charms
Formatting by Luis A. Roman

All rights reserved and return to the author. This book and parts thereof may not be reproduced in any form, stored in a retrieval system, or transmitted in any form by any means –electronic, mechanical, photocopying, or otherwise -without prior written permission of the author and publisher, except as provided by the United State of America copyright law. The only exception is by a reviewer who may quote short excerpts in a review.

Chapter One

Manuel Batista pushed open the door to the recreational vehicle park office. A tarnished copper bell tinkled overhead. Glancing up, he grinned at the old-fashioned greeting.

He'd known he would like this place when he'd first seen the name—*El Mar y El Cielo*—The Sea and The Sky. The simple name coupled with the antique bell felt like home—at least a temporary home from Chicago's icy winter.

He crossed to the counter and expected a clerk, but the tiny office was empty. Looking around, he realized the place had seen better days. Even for an RV park, the office was rundown.

A single, unvarnished counter ran the length of the room, holding a battered-looking guest book and yet another antique—a black dial phone. A vinyl-upholstered chair with a rip in the seat occupied the far corner. And tucked beneath one window was an anemic-looking plant with drooping yellowish-green leaves.

He wondered if anyone was around. The door had been unlocked. He opened his mouth and then promptly shut it when a spate of Spanish curse words singed his ears.

"*¡Carajo! ¡Coño! ¡Maldita sea!*"

If he didn't know better, he'd think he was at one of his construction sites. The only difference was the lilt of the voice, which was decidedly feminine.

An arched doorway behind the counter opened into a back room. He leaned over the countertop and craned his neck. But he wasn't prepared for what he saw.

Faded Levi's pulled taut over the sweetest heart-shaped ass he'd seen in a month of Sundays. The object of his admiration stood bent over a cabinet shuffling through manila folders and muttering.

"Take your time, *querida*, take your time," he murmured.

Faded-blue fabric, snug as a second skin, hugged her hips and bottom, tapering down over slender legs. He could watch for hours—the view was exceptional from where he stood.

Eager to see more, he dug his elbows into the counter and angled his body forward. A loud crack followed with a shuddering groan. Beneath his elbows, the wooden counter shifted, tilting to one side. Jumping back, he realized it was too late. With a splintering crash the boards crumpled in the middle.

He bit back a choice retort. From the backroom, a dog started barking.

The woman straightened and turned around, her eyebrows arched and her eyes wide. She stared at him, her mouth open.

1

Her gray-green eyes, dotted with golden flecks, held his gaze. Embarrassed at what he'd done, he lowered his eyes, but his gaze dropped to her lush, caramel-colored lips. Then he shifted his focus from her face only to notice her long, russet-colored hair, falling in soft curls to her shoulders.

And her body. *Por Dios*, he didn't even want to go there.

With a sheepish grin, he finally met her gaze. But his face flushed, and he felt like a teenager on his first date. "*Lo siento*—I'm sorry."

"Doesn't matter." She waved her hand and then lowered it, smoothing back her auburn curls.

He shouldn't have leaned on the counter. It had been a stupid mistake—a case of too much testosterone and too little common sense. And he shouldn't have been ogling her, either. He'd thought that part of him was dead and buried.

"But I broke your counter," he said. "Sometimes I don't realize how big I am."

A mischievous gleam lit her eyes, sparking the golden nuggets in their depths. Boldly, she looked him up and down.

"You are a big one," she agreed. "But it was rotten anyway." Throwing up her hands, she said, "The whole place is rotten!"

"I, ah, I guess I..." He stopped.

She must be an employee of the Park. But he found it strange she would disparage the place to a prospective customer.

He extended his hand. "I'm Manuel Batista, and I'd like to rent a space for the winter."

She ignored his outstretched hand and pursed her lips.

He dropped his hand. "I'm a carpenter. I'll replace your counter."

Her eyes narrowed and swept over him again. He squirmed under her scrutiny, feeling like a homeless guy at a five-star resort.

"I don't give spaces for work. Only cash."

Who did she think he was? A beggar? He meant to pay for his space and replace the counter he'd ruined. His back stiffened and he stood a little taller. He reached for his wallet. "How much for three months?"

She glanced at his bulging billfold, and her skeptical look faded. "The rate's three-fifty a month for a concrete slab with electricity. For three months, you get a price break, nine hundred dollars. What kind of rig do you have?"

"A 1957 Airstream."

"Oh." Her features took on that pinched look again. "You won't need the slab."

"Nope, but I'll take the best you've got."

He counted out eight hundreds and two fifties and handed them to her. Nodding stiffly, she took the bills and tucked them in her pocket.

"I'm *Señora* Reyes, the owner of the Park. Please sign the book."

Gazing at the shattered pile of wood where the counter had been, he shook his head. The tattered volume, along with the old black phone, lay on the floor among the splintered ruins.

"Oh, sorry." She kneeled to retrieve the book.

He bent down and grabbed for the book at the same time. His fingers brushed hers. A jolt of white-hot heat, like biting into a *habañero* pepper, shot through him, making his mouth water and his cock stiffen.

Stumbling back, he managed to retain his hold on the guest book, clinging to it with the ferocious tenacity of a novice sky diver gripping a rip cord.

Since he'd sworn off women, he'd thought he hadn't missed that part of his life. Hard to believe, but he'd been celibate for over five years. Who would have thought? But now, it was as if he'd never taken that long-ago vow. And he'd never felt like this before, like he wanted to grab this woman and drag her off to bed, caveman style. What demon had infested his middle-aged body?

Straightening, he kept a tight grip on the book. He moved to the only part of the counter left standing and filled in the necessary information. When he came to the line for the length of his visit, he hesitated, though he'd already paid for three months.

The Park with its evocative name and ocean view had drawn him—not *Señora* Reyes. He glanced quickly at her left hand and found her ring finger bare. But she'd said *Señora*. She must be widowed or divorced.

He stopped himself short. Where was he going with this? He was a *grandfather*, for Chrissake, not some young hot blood.

He handed her the guest book. "I want to replace your counter. It's my responsibility."

"Not really. It was..." She lifted one shoulder. "Everything needs to be fixed. I have someone coming tomorrow to do repairs. And besides, you're a guest."

"Are you sure? I'd like to help."

"No, no, *por favor*, I'll take care of it." The corners of her generous mouth lifted in a smile. "Welcome to *El Mar y El Cielo*. I hope you have a pleasant stay. Your space is number fifty-seven. If you forward mail from home, I'll keep it in the office until you pick it up."

He nodded and retreated to the door, his hand on the doorknob. So she was the owner of the Park.

The setting sun cast a lone sunbeam through the small window, tangling in her hair and igniting the red highlights. A sultry shiver meandered down his spine. He fisted his hands, fighting the overpowering rush to comb his fingers through her hair and kiss her generous mouth.

Por Dios, what was wrong with him?

***

Catalina Reyes watched Manuel Batista cross to the Dodge Ram pickup hitched to his Airstream trailer. She seldom saw any of the old Airstreams. Most recreational vehicle owners favored luxurious Fleetwood Coaches or roomy Gulf Stream Tour Masters.

Somehow he didn't look like the Fleetwood type. Not Manuel Batista. Standing well over six feet, he was a big bear of a man with huge, muscular forearms and shoulders so wide they'd filled her doorway.

Glimpsing him for the first time, towering over the wrecked counter had been a little scary, especially after what had happened at Christmas.

But the look in his eyes had calmed her fears. She'd seen the look before—frank admiration laced with desire. She could handle that. And *Señor* Batista did have nice eyes, big and round and velvety brown. Reassuring eyes, warm and unclouded like her Lab's.

She shook her head. What was wrong with her, thinking about a strange man and how his eyes made her feel. Was she going "potty" in her middle age, as her daughter liked to say?

No, she was fine. But there was something about him... She tilted her head and considered. Not anything she couldn't deal with, of course. So long as he wasn't a deadbeat. But he'd paid in cash.

Delving into her pocket, she retrieved his money and dropped it into the cash drawer. Smoothing her hands over the wrinkled bills, she wished they were thousand-dollar notes instead of hundreds and fifties.

Thinking about money—or rather her lack of it—brought her full circle. Back to what she'd been doing when her newest customer destroyed the counter. She'd been looking for her plat and deed. Without them, she'd be hard-pressed to lodge a tax appeal.

Money—some people said it was the root of all evil. She wouldn't go that far but just when she could see the light at the end of the tunnel, the County had reassessed her property and quadrupled the taxes.

She stared at the counter, bitterly registering the collapsed and splintered wood. Another item to add to her list. She'd delayed repairs for several years, trying to pay off her house mortgage and help her kids through college. But as the place got more rundown, her occupancy rate slipped. The busy winter season was already underway and the camp was only half full.

She'd finally sold her home in Brownsville and had planned to pay for the renovations from the proceeds, but she didn't know if the price of her modest home would cover the Park's repairs, much less the increase in taxes.

Sighing, she turned back to the filing cabinet to look for her papers. For over six years she'd struggled to realize her dream, almost losing her family along the way.

And in the end, she'd lost Nieto anyway. Now it was as if she was starting over again, her future as insecure as before.

Pawing through the cabinet, she found an old legal folder. Unsnapping the rubber band, her hopes took a sharp upward turn, only to be quashed as she realized the moldy folder held ancient bank statements.

¡Perdición! Where were her documents?

Frustration, liberally laced with fear, fueled her temper. A lump formed in her solar plexus, a burning lump, like a bad case of indigestion. Her stomach twisted and her heart pinched. Afraid and angry, she kicked the cabinet door shut and fell to the floor groaning in pain. Her toes throbbed in her well-worn canvas tennies.

Feeling sorry for herself, she sat cross-legged on the floor, cradling her foot and cursing her bad luck.

***

Manuel stuck his head out the pickup window, gauging the width of the concrete slab. Backing up slowly so the Airstream wouldn't jack-knife, he yanked the steering wheel left and then right and left again. After some maneuvering, he managed to position the trailer precisely over the middle of the slab, leaving ample room for the collapsible steps.

He turned off his truck and got out, circling the trailer to check the stabilizers and the pressure in his rig's tires. Satisfied, he uncoupled the Airstream.

The Park was half empty. Even so, he had neighbors. Slot number fifty-six held a sleek Holiday Rambler Motor Coach. On the other side, berth fifty-eight stood vacant. There were two other neighbors across the way, one a refurbished camper and the other, an older-model Blue Bird Coach.

Opening up the guts of his trailer, he cut the generator and hooked up the electricity. Then he topped off the water storage and drained his septic tank. Wiping his hands on a rag, he stood back and surveyed his home on wheels.

When he heard approaching voices, he glanced around. The Holiday Rambler neighbors, an older couple, approached, smiling and waving. He'd wondered how long it would take them to greet him. This was his first real vacation, but he'd taken shorter trips and found the motor-coaching crowd to be a friendly bunch, always ready to socialize and help each other out.

Bob and Madge Decker were no exception, he soon learned, after they introduced themselves and told him they were from Iowa. He explained he was from Chicago. They were all down for the winter and would return north in the spring.

Madge gave him a rundown on the neighbors across the way. They were out for the day, but she promised to bring them around for introductions later. He chatted with the Deckers for a few minutes and then they parted company, promising to get together soon.

The elderly couple strolled to their RV, hand in hand. The purple velvet of nightfall served as a perfect backdrop. Manuel watched them, a lump forming in his throat.

Since Lydia's untimely death, twilight had been a lonely time for him—a time when the day's work was done and the night stretched long and empty. He sighed and dropped his head.

But after a few minutes of gazing at his feet, he lifted his head and rolled his shoulders. Enough self-pity. When Lydia had been alive, he hadn't appreciated her. If anything, his loneliness was a fitting penance.

But he wasn't just missing his late wife. What was he doing here—hundreds of miles from home? He'd covered a vast stretch of highways, separating him from his children and grandchildren. Did he think the simple act of moving would give his life meaning or change the past?

Lydia and he hadn't had time to spend three months on vacation. They'd had children to raise and a business to build from scratch. Now he had the time and money, but he was alone. His happiest moments had been with Lydia, even if he hadn't realized it then.

And he didn't want any quickie, cheapie relationship to fill the hollow space. He was done with that. The next time, if there was a next time, he'd know how to take care of a woman, how to appreciate her, with his heart and soul and...body.

***

The bell tinkled. Catalina scrambled to her feet. It was bad enough her office was a shambles. She didn't want a prospective customer to find her grubbing around on the floor.

Peering over the broken counter, she saw a late-model white sedan sitting in the driveway. The stenciled-on lettering identified the vehicle as belonging to the County. Even without the clue, she would have bet the short, balding man, wearing thick, black glasses and a shabby suit, wasn't a customer.

She pasted a smile on her face. "Yes, what can I do for you?"

He glanced down at the papers in his fist. "Are you Mrs. Reyes, the owner of this...?" His gaze swept the splintered pile of wood, and he clucked his tongue. "Of this...er, establishment?"

"Yes, I'm Mrs. Reyes, and I own the Park."

"My name is Clarence Fielder." He didn't offer his hand, which was a good thing because she really didn't want to shake it. "I work for the County Licensing Board. We've had complaints about your Park. If you don't mind, I'll just go over them with you." He shuffled the papers and cleared his throat. "Violation one, perimeter fence is—"

"Mr. Fielder," she cut him off, "I can read. If you'll just leave the papers, I'll take care of it." She wiped her perspiring hands on her jeans. "I have a contractor coming tomorrow to make renovations."

He lifted his head and glanced around the office again, scrutinizing its contents as if he were at a traders' market. He pushed the heavy glasses higher on his nose and made a strange snorting noise.

"All right, Mrs. Reyes, as you wish." He pursed his lips and handed her the papers. "You have thirty days to clear up said violations or you will be faced with a stiff fine and have your license revoked until the repairs are completed."

A fine—money she didn't have—on top of having her license revoked, meaning she'd have to refund money to her customers who'd already paid for the winter. More money she didn't have. She groaned under her breath, realizing this was the last straw. She'd have to borrow money against the Park and have a mortgage hanging over her head. Not to mention the increase in taxes.

She wanted to collapse in a huddled heap on the floor again, but she couldn't—no *wouldn't*—give into self-pity. She threw back her shoulders. "All the repairs will be complete in thirty days, Mr. Fielder, you have my word."

He placed his hand on the doorknob. "I don't need your word, Mrs. Reyes, I'll be back to see for myself." He glanced at the counter again.

"It just broke today."

"Well, the counter isn't on the list, but I would strongly suggest you get it replaced."

"I'd planned on it," she replied softly, gritting her teeth to keep from telling him exactly where he could put the splintered wood.

***

A confetti-colored dawn backlit Manuel's first good look at the RV Park. His professional eye, honed over three decades of experience, confirmed what *Señora* Reyes had said—the whole place was rotting to the ground.

For starters, the perimeter fence was mostly down, leaving the Park open to the highway. Inside the Park many of the utility poles were missing, rendering slots unusable. The laundry room's floor contained two gaping holes, along with one working washer and two dryers perched precariously on the edge of the fractured slab. One lone picnic area boasted a table and benches. The rest were empty slabs except for some crumbling brick barbecue pits.

Why had *Señora* Reyes allowed the Park to fall into disrepair? It was a miracle she managed to keep the place half full.

He should know because he'd done some comparison shopping, and her rates weren't that much cheaper. Scattered along the highway were lots of posh RV camps with swimming pools and clubhouses and even tennis courts.

But they all possessed one flaw. They were either on the *Laguna Madre* side of the island, facing inland, or a couple of blocks from the ocean. Only *El Mar y El Cielo* stood alone and unique in its location, commanding the end of a road called *Boca Chica* on a bluff overlooking the Gulf of Mexico.

Sloughing along the sandy trail to the top of the bluff, he paused on the precipice and gazed out to the Gulf. The horizon stretched as far as he could see, shading into a lazy haze.

He took a deep breath, filling his lungs with salty air. The soothing purr of breaking waves beat their slow measure on the sandy shore. An unfamiliar peace settled over him, quieting the thud of his heart and slowing his breath.

How many times had he dreamed of coming south for the winter and returning to his roots? It was a long-held goal finally accomplished. But even in such a scenic spot, he didn't really know what to do with his self-imposed idleness.

He was accustomed to life in the fast lane. Owning a construction business had definite perks, but idleness wasn't one of them. He'd spent his life working long hours to make his company successful.

And Pablo, his eldest son, was more than eager to take over the business. Not that he could blame his son. He was an ambitious young man with lots of new ideas. Manuel understood, but sometimes, letting go wasn't easy, especially since he was a long way from full retirement.

At his son's urging, he had tried to cut back his hours and take time to relax. He'd taken lessons in golf and tennis. But despite high-priced coaches, neither sport had appealed. Sports, other than spectator sports, weren't really his thing.

No, he preferred doing what he'd done all his life, working with his hands. So he'd bought an old Airstream and fixed it up. And come south for the winter, which wasn't much of a sacrifice because the construction business was slow in Chicago during the snowy winter months. He'd told himself he'd be better off, down here in the warm weather, rather than glued to a television set. And he'd brought his woodworking tools.

But hobbies couldn't fill the loneliness. And what did he know about vacations? Vacations were a rich man's prerogative.

Hearing an engine roar to life, he turned around. A green Ford pickup with the words: *"Torres Remodeling"* on the side exited the RV's front drive and turned onto the highway. Watching the pickup speed away, he couldn't help but feel irked she'd refused his help. For her sake, he hoped Torres would do a good job.

But the state of her repairs wasn't any of his business. She'd refused him, so he was off the hook. It wouldn't do him any good to think about the broken counter...or about her.

He'd tossed and turned last night, not really sleeping. He'd told himself it was because he was excited to finally be here but that was a bald-faced lie. No, his excitement stemmed from quite a different source—his sexy landlady.

If he weren't painfully aware of how many candles his eldest daughter, Rita, had put on his last birthday cake, he'd think he had an adolescent crush. Either that, or he'd returned to his old juvenile ways.

Shaking his head, he put her out of his mind and concentrated on what he'd come for. He descended the sandy path and walked along the beach searching for driftwood. With the dawn came the high tide—the best time to find interesting pieces.

After his morning walk, he'd unhitch his pickup and locate a grocery store and gas station. Then he'd find the Brownsville post office to forward his mail. In a few days, he'd need to go to the RV office and pick it up.

That brought him full circle again—back to *Señora* Reyes. He'd have to see her to get his mail. Thinking about seeing her, a wave of giddy anticipation swept over him, only to be drowned in the undertow of embarrassment. He refused to make a silly ass of himself again, staring at her and getting all hot and bothered.

Why couldn't he enjoy the first real vacation he'd had in years? He should make plans with the Deckers and meet his neighbors. Find some driftwood and work with it. Stay too busy to be lonely—that was the answer.

He'd read brochures about "winter Texans" and knew the senior centers in the various Valley towns offered activities for part-time residents. Unfortunately, bingo and square dancing smacked of the blue-haired set. And he wasn't quite there...yet.

But there were other things he could do. He could cross the river to México and look up his relatives. He still had an aunt and several cousins living in Matamoros.

Climbing the first dune, he glanced around. Sea grapevines covered the sand and a few tufts of sawgrass waved in the wind. He descended one hill and then scrambled to the top of the next, his tennis shoes filling with grit. From the top of the dune, he glimpsed a twisted log with several outstretched branches.

He slid down the slippery, shifting sand and stopped to kneel down, smoothing his hand over the misshapen wood. Thinking about the image he could coax from the twisted wood, he put the log into a net bag strapped to his back.

A voice drifted to him on the breeze—a high-pitched, angry voice. Straightening, he strained to hear and realized the voice came from down the beach.

He heard the Spanish curse words before he saw who was speaking. But he didn't need to see—he'd know the voice anywhere. It belonged to *Señora* Reyes. He backtracked and retreated to the last dune, watching as she threw a stick into the water for a black Labrador. He remembered the barking dog at the RV office and guessed the Lab must be hers.

But why was she angry? She'd been swearing yesterday when he'd entered the office. Now she was cursing out loud again. The woman had one hot temper.

Hot temper…or hot nature. The thought slammed into him, giving rise to a vision of twisted sheets and *Señora* Reyes' sweat-slicked, naked body writhing beneath him.

Groaning, he dragged his thoughts out of the gutter and turned away, not wanting to add to the aching stiffness of his erection by watching her perfect heart-shaped ass sashay down the beach.

But curiosity got the better of him, and he faced the ocean again. She paced the curl line of the water, cursing and tossing a stick for the Lab. When the dog fetched the stick, she leaned down and stroked his ebony fur. It was obvious she wasn't mad at the Lab.

So what was wrong? Not that he should care. In fact, he should turn around and go back the way he'd come. Too bad his feet wouldn't obey his better intentions. Not to mention the rest of his body.

Knowing himself for three dozen kinds of a fool, he half-slid down the dune and walked toward her. "Can I help?" he called out. "Is something the matter?"

Her head jerked up and her gray-green eyes widened. Eyes he could drown in, eyes the exact color of the Gulf water surging around her bare feet.

She covered her mouth with one hand and turned her back on him.

The Lab returned with the stick, jumping up and placing his paws on her shoulders, offering the piece of wood.

"Good, *Migo*, good dog." She patted his head, taking the stick from his jaws and tossing it on the ground. "Come, *Migo*, heel, it's time to go home."

The dog dropped to all fours and glanced at the discarded stick, whining. She ignored her pet's pained look and started down the beach. The Lab, obviously well-trained, followed.

Manuel watched them climb the path to the bluff, feeling like the biggest buffoon this side of the border. He remembered how she hadn't taken his hand when he'd introduced himself. And how prickly she'd been about him paying. Not to mention all the cursing and swearing.

She must be one unhappy woman.

Chapter Two

"I'm fine. Everything is fine, Carlos," Catalina lied to her son. "You worry too much, *mi hijo*."

"I don't know if I believe you, *Mamá*. I can't help but worry after what happened at Christmas."

"That was an isolated incident," she argued. "I've been running the Park for years and nothing has happened before."

"But it could happen again, with all those strangers coming and going. I don't want you to keep the Park. You've had a really good offer—an offer that would make you rich."

Why did the younger generation think money solved everything? Yes, she needed money to keep her dream alive. If she sold, she'd have plenty of money. But what would she live for? Her son didn't understand. Though, to be fair, she knew he loved her and only wanted what he thought was best.

"I don't want to be rich," she said.

"Why not? Then you wouldn't have to worry about anything."

If she stopped worrying, she might as well be dead.

"You could travel and—"

"Come see my grandchildren?"

Carlos groaned. "*Mamá*, don't you ever stop? I'm not ready to get married. I've only been out of college for a year. Talk to Alba, she's older."

"Then you should understand how I feel. You're not ready to get married, and I'm not ready to give up the Park. And even though she's older, your sister might never have children." Catalina sighed.

"You know Alba's wrapped up in her painting," she added. "But that's her choice, and I try to respect it."

"Then why pressure me?"

She blew out her breath. "I'm not pressuring you. I was trying to make a point. We all do what we're comfortable with. And I don't want to go traipsing around the world like a...like a gypsy. Wouldn't you worry about me traveling alone?"

"Traveling isn't like that nowadays—there are cruises and guided tours where you meet interesting people."

"Translation—wealthy people of my same age. Right?"

"What's wrong with that?"

Her stomach churned and the tips of her ears grew warm. She knew the signs. If they kept this up, she'd lose her temper, and she didn't like to get angry with her children. "Nothing's wrong about it for someone else. Not for me."

"Okay, *Mamá*, you win. For now."

"Speaking of Alba, how is your sister?"

"She's fine."

"Does she like her new job?"

Her two children were so different. Carlos was the analytical one. He'd majored in business and was a financial analyst at an oil and gas firm in Houston. Alba had always been artistic and eccentric.

She'd studied design and though she was committed to her career, she'd had difficulty finding a job suited to her talents. Currently, she was working for a department store chain in women's fashion, also in Houston.

"Yeah, I guess Alba likes her new job," Carlos said.

"You don't know? Don't you have Sunday dinner together?"

Knowing her children lived in the same city and kept in touch comforted her. Made her feel they looked after each other, even if it was wishful thinking on her part.

"She's canceled the past two times," Carlos said. "She's got a new boyfriend."

Alba was long past due for a serious relationship. But then times were different. Kids married later.

"I'll have to call and get the lowdown on her new love," she said.

Carlos laughed. "You do that, *Mamá*. I'm sure Alba will be excited to give you the rundown."

Fat chance, Catalina thought, and her son knew it. Carlos was open and forthright, but Alba valued her privacy, keeping most things to herself, especially personal matters.

"Thanks for calling, *m'ijo*, but we should get off. I don't want to run up your bill."

"I'm calling from my cell."

"Isn't that more expensive?"

"Not if you have unlimited minutes."

Her children were so twenty-first century while she was still mired in the last millennium. She didn't own a cell phone, though she could see the advantage. But having another bill to pay stopped her.

Carlos and Alba didn't know how good they had it. Educated and with professional jobs, living in the city. When she and Nieto were first married they couldn't even afford a telephone.

"Have you tried the computer I gave you?" Carlos asked.

She crossed her fingers behind her back. "Sure, it's great."

"Yeah, right. I bet you haven't even turned it on. You still have the password I set up for you?"

"Of course, I've got it written down. I won't lose it."

"Okay, I'll show you how to get on again if you've forgotten. I'll try to come see you next month."

"I'd like that. And bring your sister with you."

"I'll try, but you know Alba. She has a mind of her own."

"I know you can convince her."

He chuckled. "*Adios, Mamá.* I love you."

"I love you, too. *Adios.*"

She replaced the receiver and perched the phone on the rickety crate. Torres had arrived yesterday at dawn, literally rousing her from bed. He'd lost no time tearing down the splintered counter and gutting parts of her office. Then he'd roared off, muttering something about getting lumber, but he still hadn't returned. Thinking about Torres made her furious, constricting her chest so she couldn't breathe. She took a deep breath.

Let it go.

She didn't have time to be angry. And besides, she'd already gotten it out of her system on the beach. Closing her eyes, she took several more deep breaths, and the tight bands around her chest slowly loosened

Feeling better, she opened her eyes and decided what to do next. Since the remodeling was on hold, she might as well tackle her other problem—taxes. And Carlos had given her an idea. She rummaged through the closet and found the laptop he'd given her. It was his old one, but there was nothing wrong with it.

He'd wanted the latest and greatest, a notebook or tablet or something. He'd said his new computer was much faster, as if he was talking about a racecar. Of course, what she knew about computers wouldn't fill a teacup. And she didn't have a month to wait to learn. But she knew where to go.

She grabbed her purse and the computer case. She'd finally found her plat and deed, and she stuffed them in her purse. Then she hung a "closed" sign on the front door.

With a bit of luck, she wouldn't lose any customers. Rentals this winter had been slow. Still, she hated to leave it unattended. She'd often dreamed of hiring a part-time clerk.

Dreams are nice—so long as you don't expect them to come true.

***

Catalina crossed Elena Jiménez's front yard. Elena, her oldest and dearest friend, still lived in the bungalow next door to Catalina's former home.

Not much had changed in the 'hood since she'd sold her house. Dotted with small, white stucco houses set on jewel-green lawns, Brownsville's west side had retained its modest but respectable appearance. Catalina believed it was a testament to the neighborhood's close-knit Latino families.

Sometimes she missed the old 'hood and wished she lived closer to Elena. Her memories were bittersweet, filled to the brim with family life. Memories of her children playing in the sprinkler, and Nieto spinning her around the kitchen to a Mexican polka.

But that part of her life was over. Her children were grown, and she'd lost Nieto even before he'd had his stroke. When her life had been falling apart, Elena had been a rock—always there to help or lend a shoulder to cry on.

She shook her head. No time to get maudlin. She needed to put on a happy face. And not a moment too soon. Before she could knock, Elena's front door flew open and her friend grabbed her in a big hug.

"*¿Amiga, como está?*" Elena welcomed her. "I saw you drive up and I was so excited. It's been too long. You don't come around enough."

Catalina hugged Elena. "*Es verdad.* The Park keeps me busy." She released her friend and stepped back.

Elena looked the same, silver-haired and plump, attired in an embroidered Mexican dress. "I've missed you, too," Catalina said. "I guess I should have called first, but I wanted to see you and—"

"I'm glad you came, *amiga*." Elena waved her hand, dismissing Catalina's protests. "And you don't need to call. You're always welcome." Taking Catalina's arm, she pulled her toward the kitchen. "Come and sit down."

Elena clucked her tongue. "Still so skinny, my nervous friend. Come to the kitchen and I'll fatten you up. I've got *flan* and *pan dulce*. Take your pick."

"You never quit trying to make me eat, do you?"

"No, I enjoy the challenge." Elena laughed.

Catalina sank into one of the vinyl-covered kitchen chairs.

"*Café?*" Her friend asked.

"*Sí*, that would be nice."

"And...?" Elena prompted.

"Okay, okay, give me some *pan dulce*. I haven't had any in years."

"Probably not since you moved."

"Probably not."

"That's because you surround yourself with *gringos*. What do they know about *pan dulce*?"

"Not all my 'snowbirds' are *gringos*. I have a new one from Chicago, and he's Latino."

As soon as the words left her mouth, she wanted to beat her head on Elena's chipped Formica table. Why had she brought him up?

She'd told herself she wasn't going to think about her new renter, much less tell her best friend. Elena was too curious by far and like Catalina's children, thought she shouldn't run the RV Park by herself. Translation—Elena wanted her to date and remarry. Which might be the real reason she didn't visit more often, even though she missed their long, gossipy talks.

Manuel Batista. Just thinking about his sudden appearance on the beach yesterday made her flush with embarrassment. She'd been upset at Torres and venting her anger. What must her new renter think? Every time he saw her she was cursing like a drunken sailor.

Elena placed a heaping plate of sweetbread on the table and poured Catalina a cup of coffee. "That's the first time you've mentioned a man since Nieto died."

Catalina spooned in sugar and stirred her coffee. "Aren't you exaggerating? I've mentioned plenty of my deadbeat renters."

"You know what I mean. Could this one be different?"

"Don't get your hopes up. I'm done with men."

Their gazes met. Catalina took a bite of the sugary bread and a sip of her coffee. "This is so good."

Elena nodded. "How are Alba and Carlos?"

Catalina slumped in her chair, relieved her friend hadn't pressed her. The discussion naturally turned to their children, and they caught up on all the news since the last time they'd visited. But after her third coffee, Catalina felt the time slipping away. She needed to get back to the Park.

Elena lifted the coffeepot. "Another cup?"

Catalina shook her head and smiled. "I can't. I'm swimming already." Reaching across the table, she patted her friend's hand. "And I have to confess, I didn't come just to visit."

"Oh?"

"I need your help."

"Anything—just ask."

"Could you show me how to use my computer? Carlos gave me his old one." She took a folded piece of paper out of her pocket. "He gave me this password, but I don't know how to even begin. Do you mind?"

Elena's husband, Alberto, owned a string of auto repair shops. A few years ago, he'd brought home a computer for his business. The machine had fascinated Elena, and she'd spent hours learning it. Over time, she'd mastered her husband's administrative work and graduated to the Internet.

Elena clucked her tongue again. "You've never used a computer, have you? I don't know how you've managed without one."

"I keep all my records by hand. I never saw the need."

"Computers aren't just for work, you know. You could email your kids." Elena's eyes lit up. "Or better yet, check up on them on Facebook."

Catalina combed her fingers through her hair. "I don't want to spy on them like that."

"Why not? Everything they post is for anyone to see."

"Really? That's crazy, why would anyone want to do that?"

Elena shook her head. "Never mind. Where's your computer?"

Catalina zipped open the soft computer case and lifted out the laptop. She sat it on Elena's kitchen table and plugged in the battery cord. She remembered Carlos showing her how to do that. Then she opened the laptop lid and stared at the blank screen.

Elena leaned over her and pushed a button above the keyboard. A multi-colored screen lit up after a few seconds. Then her friend hit the enter key, and a box, asking for a password, appeared.

"Did you see what I did?" Elena pushed the button again. "Now you do it and type in your password."

Feeling like a kid in school, Catalina mimicked what her friend had done and then typed in the password. The computer's screen changed and a picture of a sunset appeared, overlain with tiny boxes of letters and symbols along the left-hand side and bottom.

Step-by-step, Elena showed her around the computer, explaining how to get on the Internet and what some of the buttons led to, including a blank place for writing, along with something that looked like a gigantic spreadsheet, which her friend called Excel.

Despite her initial doubts, Catalina was intrigued.

"Do you have a Wi-fi connection at the Park?" Elena asked.

Catalina lifted her head. "Wha—what? Oh, yes, I do. I had to subscribe because my renters demanded it. The competition, you know. All the RV Parks and motels have the Internet now."

Elena nodded and showed Catalina how to connect to her home's Internet. Then she explained to Catalina how to connect to her own Wi-fi at the Park, using the key code she gave to her renters. Elena pulled over a chair, and they spent almost an hour getting Catalina comfortable with the computer.

"Is there anything in particular you want to find?" her friend asked.

"Cameron County property valuations and tax information for the other RV Parks on Boca Chica Road. Do you know how to do that?"

"Sure. Alberto has me check our properties from time to time. Doing a little comparison shopping?"

"You might say that. The County just quadrupled my taxes."

"Oh, no, Catalina—you're kidding?"

"I wish I was."

"Do you have the legal description with you?"

"*Sí*, I thought you might need it." Catalina opened her purse and retrieved the plat and deed.

"*Bueno.* Watch what I look up. Take notes if you want."

A few minutes later, her friend had found the information. And what they'd found infuriated Catalina. Other RV Parks of approximately the same size were valued at one-third of what her Park was, and they paid a fraction of the taxes.

"This doesn't look right." Elena shook her head.

"I know. That's why I wanted to do some research before I lodged an appeal."

"Let me get a copy from my computer; it's hooked to our printer." Elena got to her feet and patted Catalina's shoulder. "You should think about investing in a good printer."

Catalina rolled her eyes.

Elena chuckled. "Well, one step at a time. At least you know how to get on your computer. It's a start."

Catalina stared at the screen and scrolled through the tax rolls. In a few minutes, Elena returned with several pieces of paper stapled together. "Here you go. When did your taxes go up?"

"I just got the notice, after the first of the year."

"But it doesn't make sense, and it's not fair."

"A new developer came by before Thanksgiving and offered me double what Yolanda was offered. Just like the others, he wants to build a high-rise condominium complex with an ocean view." Catalina turned off her computer and put it and the papers in the carry-all.

Elena loosed a low whistle. "That's a lot of money."

"Yeah, SpaceX coming to town has boosted everyone's property values." She shook her head. "Mine more than others, it would seem."

"You need an attorney, Catalina."

"I might *need* one, but I can't afford one."

"Alberto has a friend who would be willing to help out. He does our legal work."

"*Gracias*, but I can't pay him."

"Don't worry about it. He's on retainer."

"I can't take your charity, *amiga*, because I don't know when I'll be able to pay you back."

Elena put her arms around Catalina. "Don't think of it as charity. Think of it as one friend helping another." Drawing back, she held Catalina at arm's length. "*Por favor*, just talk to him. For me." Elena wagged her finger. "Remember, we're all connected and there will come a time when I need a favor from you. You'll see."

What Elena said was true. They were connected because they cared about each other. Sighing, she capitulated. "All right. I'll talk to him. But if this turns out to be a long and drawn-out legal battle, I don't want to impose."

"Just talk to him." Elena squeezed her shoulders. "I'll get you his card. And I'll call and let him know you're coming." She hesitated and then grinned. "And I might mention he's single—divorced—and nice looking."

"Elena, please, don't play matchmaker. I've got my hands full without dating."

"Oh, all right. I just thought you could mix a little pleasure with business."

"Thanks, but no thanks."

Her friend was irrepressible, trying to match her with men. Elena believed all Catalina had to do was find the right man and her problems would evaporate. But she'd had the right man, Nieto, for over twenty-five years. Or she'd thought he was the right man until that last year. She sniffed and swallowed hard.

Now all she wanted was to fulfill her dream and honor Yolanda's memory. No man could do that for her. She'd learned the hard way she needed to solve her own problems.

But a vision of broad shoulders and warm brown eyes danced before her; Manuel Batista again. Like a deranged boomerang, her thoughts returned to him. But why? She barely knew the man, and the two times they'd met, she'd been angry and frustrated. And he probably thought she was a dirty-mouthed witch.

She shrugged one shoulder. What did she care? Cursing was her one outlet, a way to deal with frustration. A verbal barrier she threw up to keep her fears locked out so she could face another day.

***

Manuel strode down the path to the beach. The sun, a fiery red ball, hung poised above the horizon as if reluctant to end the day. He'd fallen into a routine of walking the beach at dawn and sunset. Those were the times when the sun gilded the water and splashed the sky with a Technicolor show.

At first, he'd spent his time scouring the shore for driftwood. Now he just walked, enjoying the sea and gaudy sky. Besides, he'd already stockpiled enough driftwood to last for several weeks, though if a new and interesting piece washed up, he wouldn't turn it down. He'd managed to keep busy with his woodcarving. And to make certain he didn't get bored, he'd purchased some fishing tackle, going to a nearby pier a couple of times to try his luck.

Activity was good, but the loneliness hadn't gone away. He missed his family. Maybe the vacation had been a mistake. Maybe he wouldn't come next winter.

Thinking about his kids, he realized he might have mail at the RV office, though they'd been exchanging emails. Sometimes, his grandkids sent him hand-lettered cards. But he hesitated about getting his mail. He wasn't in any hurry to face *Señora* Reyes again after she'd snubbed him.

He hadn't seen her since that time on the beach. He'd seen the Torres remodeling truck a couple of times, but the guy didn't stay long. And nothing had been fixed around the Park, as far as he could tell. The Deckers had been talking the other day, saying they were thinking of moving. He didn't like to think of them leaving, but he could understand their reasons.

What kept him here?

Just because he'd paid in advance didn't mean he couldn't ask for his rent back. But he hated to do that to *Señora* Reyes for some reason. His son, Pablo, would say he was an old softie.

A dog barked in the distance, and he stiffened. Getting his mail was bad enough, but the last thing he wanted was another chance encounter on the beach with her.

He turned around, retracing his steps.

An eerie howl stopped him. The anguished sound of it tugged at his heart. More barking and howling followed, increasing to a frenzied pitch. The Lab must be on the other side of the next dune. Not that he could be certain it was her Lab, but he hadn't seen any other dogs around the Park. And this particular dog sounded like it was in trouble. He couldn't allow a dumb animal to suffer, no matter who the owner was.

Making up his mind, he turned around again and scaled the dune. Topping the hill, he surveyed the beach. At first, the shore appeared deserted. Then he saw movement on the other side of an industrial-sized trashcan.

He trotted onto the beach and found the black Lab hopelessly tangled in two fishing lines. No one was around. But some idiot must have been surf fishing earlier and left the poles in the sand. The Lab had run into the lines.

The dog pivoted and whirled in a tight circle, as if chasing his tail, getting more ensnared and howling the whole time.

Manuel approached the Lab cautiously. He hoped the dog wasn't vicious. Labs weren't usually, but you never knew with a dog, especially a trapped and frightened one.

Moving closer, he talked nonsense under his breath, low and slow. What was the dog's name? He tried to remember. And then the name came to him—*Migo*. Magician, strange name for a dog.

"*Migo*, boy, good boy. I want to help you." He moved slowly forward.

At the sound of his name, the Lab stopped turning and sat on his haunches, pink tongue lolling. His intelligent brown eyes followed Manuel's approach.

"That's a good boy, *Migo*. Good boy."

Migo didn't move, but the dog's eyes never left him.

"Good boy, *Migo*. Just stay still, old boy." Manuel moved closer, holding out his hand for the dog to smell. The Lab sniffed his fingers and then the palm of his hand. After a tense moment, the Lab licked him.

Manuel laughed and patted his head. "Good boy, *Migo*, now we're friends."

The dog whined and got up, trying to wag his tail.

Recalling the dog's obedient nature, Manuel commanded, "Sit, *Migo*, sit." The Lab sat down again. "Good boy, give me a minute and I'll get you loose. Just a minute, *Migo*."

Gazing at the tangle of fishing lines wrapped around the dog's body and legs, he knew what he had to do and to hell with the owner of the tackle. Whoever had left the poles deserved to have his lines cut. What if *Migo* had been a small child?

Taking out his pocketknife, Manuel sliced the lines. Then he started to untangle the plastic mess. Slowly and carefully, he freed the dog's limbs. Migo fidgeted and whined, but he stayed put.

Manuel threw the tangled ball of lines into the garbage can and set the fishing poles beside it. Crouching down, he ran his hands over the Lab's short, black fur, checking for injuries. The dog trembled at his touch, obviously impatient to be away and racing across the beach.

"Good, *Migo*, good boy, just a minute and I'm done. Then we'll take you home." The Lab appeared to be okay except for a few cuts on his hind legs where the lines had pulled tight.

He scratched the dog's ears. "Let's get you home and fix those cuts. Okay? Heel, *Migo*, heel."

A few minutes later, Manuel pushed open the front door of the A-frame office. The desk he'd demolished had disappeared. In its place were two overturned crates, one holding the phone and the other the guest book.

Glancing around, he'd have to say the place looked worse than before. Some of the cheap paneling had been torn from the wall, leaving gaping holes. And the mail slots were half gone with the remaining ones spread across the wall like a bag lady's derelict grin.

As before, the office was empty. But he knew *Señora* Reyes must be here. He hadn't been back to the office, but he'd paid attention to her habits. She ran the place by herself. And when she left, she put up a closed sign and locked the office.

He squatted down and stroked the dog's silky head. He was surprised how well-trained *Migo* was. Now the Lab was home, he'd thought the dog would bolt.

"What are you doing with my dog, *Señor* Batista?" *Señora* Reyes appeared in the doorway. "Come, *Migo*, come here."

At her command, the Lab looked confused. He gazed at Manuel and whined. Then he swung his head and glanced at his owner. His owner won out. *Migo* nuzzled Manuel's hand and thumped his tail, the equivalent of a canine apology, before moving to *Señora* Reyes' side.

Manny stepped back and almost left without answering. But then he stopped himself. This was ridiculous. He'd done her a favor, but she'd immediately gone on the offensive, making him feel like he'd done something wrong.

What was the matter with the woman? What...or who...had made her so defensive and abrasive?

Chapter Three

Catalina patted *Migo*. "What are you doing with my dog?" she asked again.

Unfortunately, she had to crane her neck to meet his gaze. He was taller than she remembered. Like one of those big Sequoias in California, he towered over her.

He spread his hands, palms out. "I found him on the beach tangled in somebody's fishing lines. I cut him loose and brought him home."

She looked him up and down and glanced at *Migo* again. Her dog appeared to be all right, and there was no reason *Señor* Batista wouldn't be telling the truth.

"*Gracias*, for rescuing *Migo*. Was anyone around?"

"Nope, didn't see anyone. Just the two poles propped in the sand."

"*¡Coño!* I wish people wouldn't do that. It's dangerous."

Her face grew warm. She covered her mouth with one hand. She'd done it again. That was the third time she'd cursed in front of *Señor* Batista.

"I agree. They shouldn't leave their poles like that."

She pulled her hand through her hair, smoothing it from her face. "I could post a sign on my property, warning people not to leave their fishing poles unattended. But I wish the State would take responsibility, since the beaches are public."

"Signs would be a good idea." He nodded and stroked his jaw. "I didn't realize the beaches were public."

"Yes, all of Padre Island's beaches are public. None are privately owned."

"That's interesting. Explains some things." He turned to go and then turned back. "You might want to look at your dog's hind legs. He got some shallow cuts from the fishing lines, but I couldn't find any other injuries."

"Yes, thank you. Umm...how did you know his name?"

"I heard you call him."

"You mean that morning on the beach?" Her face grew warm again, thinking of how she'd ignored his offer to help.

His gaze snagged hers and held, his brown eyes assessing. She knew what he was thinking, but she refused to acknowledge it. She was the way she was. And besides, for so big a man, he sure could skulk around.

Tilting her chin up, she stared back at him. And liked what she saw. Chocolate-colored eyes, a hatchet-straight nose, and a chiseled, sensuous mouth. A lock of straight brown hair fell across his forehead, lending a boyish appeal to his rugged features.

"I remember the name you used when he was fetching a stick from the water."

Though his reply was straightforward, she knew he implied more than he said. But she refused to apologize for letting off steam. What was unforgivable was she'd been so upset she'd been purposely rude. She dropped her gaze.

"You don't have to be embarrassed, *Señora* Reyes, I'm not the morality patrol."

She lifted her head and thrust out her chin. This was too much. Exchanging guarded glances was one thing but openly discussing her lapse of judgment was another.

"I'm glad, *Señor* Batista, especially since it's none of your business."

Despite her snippy reply, he grinned. "My name is Manuel. But my friends call me Manny. This *señor y señora* stuff is getting a little silly. What's your name?"

"I don't think—"

"Come on, I rescued your dog."

What could it hurt? After all, he had helped *Migo*. And she *had* been rude. So long as he didn't expect an apology, she could be civil. Remembering how she hadn't shaken his hand when he arrived, she thrust out her hand. "Nice to meet you, Manuel. I'm Catalina."

He swallowed up her hand in his huge, callused paw. At his touch, an unexpected tingle trickled down her spine. A slow seep of heat suffused her when she realized how strong and work-roughened his hand was.

"Catalina," he repeated. "I like that name. My grandmother was named Catalina." He released her hand.

"I'm glad you approve, *Señor*, uh, Manuel."

"Manny."

"Manuel," she repeated, standing firm.

His grin broadened into a smile. And when he smiled, his rough features softened and his warm eyes glowed. *Madre de Dios*, he exuded a rugged charm that was very attractive. Even more, in a strange sort of way he made her feel safe. Like he would champion her or something. He reminded her of the big bear, *Balu*, from the Disney movie, *"The Jungle Book."* She should know because her kids had watched the video until the tape wore out.

"Do you want me to hold *Migo* while you look at his legs?" he asked.

Did she want his help?

The safer course of action would be to say no. He might seem charming and safe on the surface, but she'd learned the hard way she possessed poor judgment when it came to men.

But even as well-trained as *Migo* was, she knew he'd resist having his wounds disinfected. Manuel Batista looked like he could wrestle a half-crazed steer into submission, if he wanted to.

"Yes, I could use some help," she agreed. "I'd like to put him on the kitchen counter, but I don't think I can keep him there."

"An obedient dog like *Migo*?" Manuel glanced at her pet. "He'll stay if you ask him to."

Catalina rolled her eyes. Why had Manuel offered to help if he didn't think she needed it? She had a good idea of the real reason, and it was on the tip of her tongue to tell *Señor* Smarty-Pants she'd changed her mind.

"*Migo* might be obedient but when it comes to pain, he's a big sissy. Like a lot of his gender," she couldn't help but add. "He won't want me to get within ten feet of his wounds with soap and alcohol."

Manuel frowned, but he didn't take the bait. "Not a problem. I'm glad to help. Just show me where you want him."

"Follow me." She led him into the back, through her office and into the kitchen.

"You live here?" he asked.

"Yes, I do." She threw back her shoulders, telling herself she had no reason to be ashamed.

Torres was the one who should be ashamed. He appeared to have a penchant for tearing down, but so far he hadn't started any of the necessary restoration work. He was always running off, claiming he needed more supplies, and resurfacing when she least expected him.

She'd about reached her limit. If he didn't fix something the next time he showed up, she'd fire his sorry ass. Still, she knew how awful her place must look.

Behind the reception area and tiny office, the A-frame building was one big space with an enclosed bathroom off the kitchen. The kitchen took up most of the room on the bottom floor. And it was a mess. Cabinets had been pulled from the walls and drawers were missing. There was a hole where the pantry should be. The refrigerator sat in the middle of the floor so the drywall could be taped and bedded.

Across from the kitchen was a small living area tucked into one corner where the paneling had been removed, leaving the naked drywall beneath. Upstairs was a loft bedroom that looked down into the living area. Fortunately, for her sanity, Torres hadn't touched the bathroom or bedroom yet.

Manuel opened his mouth as if he was going to say something. She caught his eye. He dropped his gaze and reached down to grab *Migo*. That was good. If he dared to say anything about how her home looked, she'd tell him to put a sock in it.

"Could you put *Migo* there?" She pointed to the counter beside the sink.

"Sure." Manuel hoisted the Lab as if he weighed no more than a cream puff.

Watching him lift her dog, Catalina couldn't help but notice the bulge of Manuel's biceps and the corded strength of the tendons in his forearms.

Her mouth went dry as sawdust. The air in the kitchen felt close. She swallowed hard and fought the urge to fan herself. Like Super Glue, her gaze was locked on his muscular arms. Not only did he look like a bear, if she were any judge, he was as strong as one.

Standing this close to his raw masculine strength, and with the soapy-clean, man-smell of him tantalizing her senses, her stomach muscles tightened. And lower, she felt the old, familiar stinging ache.

He glanced over his shoulder. "I've got him. Bring on the soap and alcohol."

She jerked her head up, and a flash of heat basted her face. She'd been daydreaming—or fantasizing.

She grabbed a bar of soap and the bottle of alcohol she kept by the sink. Then she turned on the water faucet and lathered her hands with soap. She grasped one of her dog's hind legs and worked the lather into his fur.

Migo whined and tried to wriggle away, but Manuel clamped down, holding him still and soothing him with low words.

She focused on *Migo*, not daring to look at Manuel or accidentally brush against him. After liberally soaping the cuts, she used a wet dishtowel to rinse them. Then she bent over to examine the wounds.

"They're not deep," he said.

His voice, rumbling from the expanse of his broad chest, forced her to glance up. Her gaze met his. This close, she could see the thick fringe of his eyelashes framing his brown eyes. He had a small bump in the middle of his nose. An old break—maybe from a fistfight?

But as strong as he was, she couldn't imagine him fighting. There was something innately gentle about Manuel Batista. Even the firm but tender way he held *Migo*.

A lump lodged in her throat. What she wouldn't give to be held like that. How long had it been since someone had protected and cherished her? She closed her eyes, fighting an overpowering urge to bury her face in Manuel's broad chest. And just as swiftly as the urge swept over her, she recoiled.

What was wrong with her? Had she flipped out?

Giving herself a mental shake, she poured alcohol onto the dry end of the dishtowel and smoothed the soaked cloth over her dog's back legs. "No, the cuts aren't deep. That's good."

Migo tried to twist away. But Manuel held him firmly, patting his head and telling him what a good boy he was. At his quiet words, she felt a stab of insane jealousy, wishing someone would say nice things to her. All she got was criticism from her renters and demands from the authorities. And Torres played her for a sucker.

Madre de Dios, her wits were addled. How could she be jealous of her own dog? Maybe she *had* gone around the bend. Maybe her son was right. She should sell and live a life of ease.

But it wasn't her problems that had brought on her crazy feelings. Was it?

No, it was her close proximity to this most unsettling bear of a man. She knew she should be grateful for his kind handling of her Lab, but she resented him instead. He made her acutely aware of how lonely she was. How lonely and needy.

She counted to ten, breathing slowly and stroking her dog's soft fur. "Good boy, that should do it." Nodding to Manuel, she said, "You can put him down now." She washed her hands at the sink.

Manuel placed *Migo* on the floor and patted his head. "I was wondering why you call him *Migo*—magician. It's a strange name for a dog."

"Oh, that." She chuckled and crossed to the kitchen table. *Migo*, obviously forgiving her for the soap and alcohol treatment, followed her, his tail wagging.

"It's a silly joke I made up. You see, I didn't want a dog." She shook her head. "They're like kids, a lot of trouble. But when I saw him, I fell in love with him."

Leaning down, she stroked her pet's ears. "Didn't I, old boy?" *Migo* licked her hand. She straightened and rested her fists on her hips. "It was like magic, like he cast a spell on me, so I called him *Migo*."

Manuel's gaze rested on her, an appraising gleam in his eyes. What had she said? That she'd fallen in love with a puppy. Why was that such a big deal? Or was he more perceptive than she'd thought. Did he see through her tough exterior, past her potty-mouthed swearing and realize how alone and scared she was.

Madre de Dios, she hoped not.

Affecting a nonchalant pose, she dusted her hands on her jeans. "Can I get you something? Coffee?" She bit her lip. Why had she offered? If he accepted, he'd stay.

"No, thanks," he said. "I guess I better be going."

Relief mingled with a strange sensation in the pit of her stomach. She turned away and rearranged the salt and pepper shakers on the table.

"Thanks again. I really appreciate your help." Glancing down at *Migo*, she added, "I think you've made a friend for life."

"I like dogs, especially ones as well-behaved as yours."

Was he complimenting her or her dog? Not that it mattered. She'd never play the pathetic little fool again for any man—no matter how attractive he might be.

"Well, *adios*," he said, moving to the door. Then he snapped his fingers and turned around. "I almost forgot. Do I have any mail?"

"Yes, you do."

"*Bueno*. Could I get it? I hope it's from my kids."

"You have kids?" She didn't mean to sound surprised.

"*Sí*, grown ones, and two grandchildren with another on the way."

"Me, too, I've got grown kids. But no grandchildren yet."

"Yes, but..." He paused and looked around. "Do your kids live close by?"

Inwardly, she cringed. He'd been nice so far—why did he have to ruin it? She'd told him she was in the process of remodeling. "Not that close by. Why do you want to know?" She crossed her arms over her chest.

"You don't have anyone helping you? Do you?" He hitched his thumb over his shoulder. "I noticed when you leave the Park; you put a closed sign up."

"My kids live in Houston. I'm widowed and on my own." She wanted to tell him it was none of his business, but he'd been nice with *Migo*, so she bit back the words.

"Where's the guy doing the remodeling? I haven't seen his truck."

So he was watching her, as she'd thought. At least, he'd been taking note of the comings and goings around the Park. Knowing that, she wasn't sure how she felt about it.

"Torres took off. He got a bigger job and said he'd come back later."

"That day on the beach with *Migo*?"

"*Sí*, I went a little crazy when he left my office torn apart."

"Sorry I intruded."

Uncrossing her arms, she waved off his apology. "That's okay, you didn't know." She hesitated, reluctant to ask his advice. On the other hand, she was desperate. The days were slipping by, and the County had given her a deadline. She couldn't afford to lose her license and pay a fine.

Couldn't afford to let her personal feelings get in the way of business.

"If you're a carpenter, then you've worked construction jobs," she ventured.

Glancing up, she realized she couldn't make out his features. Outside, the sun had set and her kitchen lay in shadow. In the dimness, he looked larger, even a bit intimidating. Nervous, she switched on the overhead light.

He blinked at the sudden brightness. "I've worked construction jobs all my life. I own a contracting business. My oldest son, Pablo, is taking care of it for me." He tugged on his earlobe. He had nice ears, she noticed, just the right size for his build and they lay close against his head. "There's not much work in Chicago during the winter."

TMI. More information than she needed. Why was he being so open? He wasn't like any other man she knew. He didn't boast or go on about himself. He seemed comfortable in his own skin.

"That's great," she said. "Great you know so much about construction."

Migo nuzzled her leg. Reaching down, she patted his head. Past time for his dinner. Grateful for something to do—something to take the edge off their conversation—she crossed to the corner and reached for the fifty-pound sack of dog chow.

"Here, let me do that," he said, coming up behind her.

His hand covered hers. His skin was warm and rough. She closed her eyes, remembering Nieto's calloused hands on her body, touching her in places that gave her pleasure.

Heat spiraled through her. Flushing, she jerked her hand away. "Yes, *por favor. Gracias.*His bowl is by the back door."

Nodding, he picked up the bag as if it weighed no more than a few ounces and filled the Lab's bowl. She would have dragged the heavy sack across the floor and spilled half of it. She'd forgotten what it was like to have a man around. A strong man with calloused hands.

Tail wagging, *Migo* dug into his dinner. Manuel replaced the sack in the corner and dusted his hands. "What did you want to know about the construction business?"

She stared at him, trying to regain her focus. Pushing her hair back from her face, she was acutely aware of its softness against her neck. When was the last time she'd noticed anything tactile about her body?

"I was wondering if you could explain something," she said.

"Be glad to."

"If Torres started with me, why doesn't he finish here first? I thought, first come, first served."

He chuckled. "That holds true for most things, but not construction."

She didn't take offense at his laughter, didn't think he was mocking her. Instead, she liked the sound of his laughter, rolling from deep inside his massive chest.

"Why not construction?"

"Because contractors have to go where the money is."

"But I was paying him."

"You said he got a bigger job."

"Yes. But why did he leave?"

"Because if the job is bigger, it would give him cash flow to finance other jobs."

"That's a great reason." She threw up her hands. "And it doesn't help me a bit."

"No, it doesn't." He leaned against the kitchen counter and crossed his legs at the ankle. "I don't want to make light of your problem, but cash flow is key to a small contractor. You never have enough to meet expenses and keep the shirt on your back, not until you get bigger. So you have to go after the big jobs to stay afloat."

She grimaced. "But what about my place?"

"That's a problem."

"*Sí*, one I don't need." She chewed on her lip, wondering if she was ready to take the plunge. "And if he doesn't come back soon, I'll be forced to get someone else."

Grinning, he curled his hand into a fist and pounded his chest like Tarzan. "You're looking at him."

"You'd take over the job?"

"Don't sound so surprised. I'm more than capable."

Oh, I'm sure you are, she thought as her gaze trailed over his broad, broad shoulders and massive chest, down his Adonis-shaped forearms and powerful thighs. More than capable—of that and a whole lot more.

She grabbed the coffeepot and a cup. "Are you sure you don't want some coffee?"

He shook his head. "What about my offer?"

What about his offer?

Could she stand being around him, day after day? She'd never been so drawn to a man before. So she-bitch hot for him that she shocked herself.

She spooned coffee into the filter. "I thought you were on vacation. Why would you want to take a job?"

He grabbed the carafe and filled it at the sink.

She watched him with a kind of awe. He was so nice and helpful. He'd charmed her without really trying and his body was...his body was smoking hot. He wasn't what she would call handsome, but his features were rugged and decidedly masculine. And he had a way about him that was comforting, protective even. But she'd be crazy to let him into her life. She'd sworn off men. And besides, he was a "snowbird." Visiting the Rio Grande Valley to escape the winter. After a few weeks he'd return home.

But what choice did she have? She didn't know when Torres would return. And the deadline was looming closer. She'd lose her license and the Park would close if she didn't meet the deadline.

The Park's existence and her dream, the dream she'd sacrificed everything for, would go up in smoke if she didn't act. As for resisting Manuel, she wasn't a teenager anymore. Surely she could control her hormones.

He handed her the carafe. "I want the job, Catalina." He hesitated and snagged her gaze. "I'm lonesome. This is the first time I've been away from my kids. I need to work."

He'd admitted he was lonely and missing his family.

No man ever did that. Tears sprang to her eyes, as she realized how difficult saying the words out loud must have been. And she empathized, understood exactly how he felt. Sometimes, in the darkest hours of the night, she would wake up shaking all over and wanting Nieto. Needing Nieto, despite what had happened.

With trembling hands, she poured the water into the coffeemaker and set it to brew. Closing her eyes, she counted to ten. She had to get control. It was simple, really. She needed his skills and he needed to work.

She stretched out her hand. "You've got the job. Two conditions, though, we need to agree on price, and..." She stopped and ticked off the fingers on her hands. "You have only twenty-one days to complete the Park repairs or I lose my license."

29

He took her hand and shook it. "Don't worry, you'll like my price." He released her hand and smiled a lop-sided smile. "I better get started first thing tomorrow."

Yeah, his price might be right in dollars and cents, but what would working with him on a daily basis cost her—in other ways?

Chapter Four

"Rita, *niña*, you know I'll be home in time for your baby," Manny told his eldest daughter. "I wouldn't miss seeing my grandbaby come into the world."

"Then why'd you take the job?" she asked. "You're supposed to be relaxing."

He switched the cell phone to his other ear, stalling for time. Did he dare tell her the truth? Nope, that would upset her more. He didn't know why he'd told her about the RV Park job in the first place. Something to say, he guessed, or maybe because he was excited.

"I'm not very good at vacations." He shrugged. "Used to working too hard."

"But that's why you need to relax, *Papá*. You're not getting any younger, you know."

What a thing to say. Why did young people think everyone over forty had one foot in the grave and the other on a banana peel? He appreciated her concern but the way she'd put it left a lot to be desired.

"*Papá*, are you there?"

"I'm here. But I'm having a hard time believing I'm *that* old." Especially with the way he felt about Catalina. He'd never been so hot and horny in his life. And given his past history—that was saying something.

"You know that's not what I mean." Righteous indignation flooded his daughter's voice.

"Then don't lecture me about my age, *mi hija*."

She sniffed, a small sound, but it conveyed how she felt, wrestling with her recalcitrant father. He grinned, remembering Rita's rebellious stage at thirteen. She'd sported spiked, dyed blue hair and pierced parts of herself that no God-fearing girl should know about much less alter.

And his eldest daughter was about to have her first child. Then she'd really know what it felt like to be on the other side of the fence.

"How's everybody?"

"Pablo's fine, working like a fiend, like someone else we know. And his family is great. Juan Luis says he's going to babysit for me."

His eight-year-old grandson, Juan Luis, didn't know what he was getting into. "I want to see that."

She laughed. "Maybe with a little supervision."

"How are Claudia and Ernesto."

"Buried in their jobs as usual and doing the singles scene."

His two oldest kids, Pablo and Rita, had followed in their parents' footsteps, marrying young and starting families. But his two youngest had gone to college, gotten their degrees, and found professional jobs. It was as if his family had split in two, but when the chips were down, they were all still family.

"Don't you call or email them?" she asked.

"Of course I do. But they're so busy; I usually get Pablo's wife and Claudia and Ernesto's voice mail or a really short text back, telling me they're fine."

"Meaning I'm the easy one, the pregnant housewife who has nothing better to do."

"Don't talk like that, Rita. That life was good enough for your mother."

"Times are different."

"But you wanted a family. I don't understand this sudden—"

"It's just so hard, *Papá*, trying to live on one income." He heard the frustration in her voice. "We scrimp and budget and do without, but I don't know how we will get by when the baby comes."

"You let me worry about that."

"No! Absolutely not! We can't depend on you for handouts. And I don't want to undermine Sam's self-confidence." She paused. "I've been thinking about getting a part-time job when the baby is a year old or so."

"Are you sure you want to?"

"I don't know if I *want* to, but I think I have to. So we can survive."

Manny sighed. He knew it was tough on kids today, especially ones with blue-collar jobs like his son-in-law, Sam. But then, it had been tough on him and Lydia too. His daughter was strong and resourceful; she'd do what she had to do.

But now he understood why it was so important for him to be home when she delivered her baby. His daughter was feeling vulnerable and scared, and she needed her father.

"Don't worry, *niña*, I'll finish up the job and come home. You're not due until late April."

"But the doctor says you never know with the first one."

"I'll be there, *hija mía*, you can count on me."

***

Manny hammered the last nail into the counter. Gratified at replacing what he'd destroyed, he stood back and surveyed his work. The old counter had been unvarnished rough wood. This one would be better. He would apply several layers of lacquer and put on a Formica top.

Proud of his accomplishment, he wanted to press forward and finish the reception area. He crossed to the one window and inspected the drywall behind the paneling. Then he noticed the windowsill was crumbling. Checking the window, he found it leaked. The frame was rotten and warped. Was there anything in this place that didn't need fixing?

He hoped he could meet Catalina's deadline—it was going to be tight. There was a whole lot more to do than he'd originally thought.

Catalina strode into the office, a bundle of mail in her hands. She'd rigged the remaining mail slots to correspond with the occupied spaces in the Park. The distinctive vanilla aroma of her perfume filled the small room. She smelled good enough to eat, like pound cake baking in the oven.

Noticing the new counter, she put the mail down and ran her hand over its surface. "You did this in one day?" She sounded awed.

"I'm not finished."

"But this is great."

"Just wait. You'll like it better when I finish."

"No extra charge?"

That was the one thing he didn't like—her preoccupation with money—as if she expected him to take advantage. He didn't mind her brutal honesty or colorful language. Even her occasional rudeness he could accept, but her fixation on money was frustrating. What would he have to do to gain her trust?

And he wanted to gain her trust. More than that. He wanted to date her. Date her, hell. He wanted to get into her panties. And despite the vow he'd made, he couldn't seem to stop. He'd grieved and done penance for five years. Was that enough? Was any amount of time enough?

But he and Catalina were free and single. What could a little tousle in the sheets hurt? Actually, it might take the edge off them both.

He'd told the truth when he'd asked for the job—he was lonely and missing work. But he hadn't told the whole truth. What he really wanted was to feel her curvaceous body pressed against his. Wanted to cup her perfect ass against his hard cock. And wanted to sample her generous mouth.

Por Dios, he was losing it.

Bending down, he hammered in a loose nail. And mentally pounded his horny thoughts into some semblance of restraint.

"Manuel?"

He straightened. "Manny."

"Okay, Manny, what about the counter?"

He knew what she wanted.

"No extra charge."

Gazing at her, he couldn't believe how beautiful she was without a trace of makeup. The light illuminated her perfect skin and ignited the red in her hair. "I should call you 'Red.'"

"Why?"

"Your hair for one thing." He smiled and couldn't help but tease. "And then there's the problem of your—"

"Temper," she finished and blushed.

He laughed. For a widowed lady she blushed a lot. One more reason to call her Red. And her blushing meant she wasn't as immune to him as she would have him believe. If he could harness her temper and put it to use in bed, he'd bet she'd be a tigress.

"Don't laugh." She chewed on her lip. He wished he were the one chewing on her full lips. "I've had to watch my temper all my life. It's not a lot of fun."

"No, I imagine it wouldn't be."

"And don't you dare call me 'Red.'"

Solemnly, he held up one hand. "Okay, I promise not to call you Red."

"*Bueno.* I'm glad we're clear on that." She leaned over the new counter and smiled. "What's next?"

The breath snagged in his throat. She was wearing a low-cut, hot-pink peasant blouse and when she bent over the counter, he could see her full breasts spilling over a very lacy, very sexy black bra. His loins caught fire and he could feel himself lengthening and hardening.

He couldn't tear his eyes away.

Glancing down, she must have realized she'd put herself on display because she flushed beet red again and straightened. She turned her back to him and picked up the bundle of mail, stuffing letters and circulars into the slots.

"I'm going to do the mail slots next," he said, finally answering her question.

"That's nice," she threw over her shoulder.

"I'll finish the office first. Then I'll work on your perimeter fence or your laundry room. You decide which one."

That got her attention. She pivoted around, her eyes wide. "Wow! I get to decide. I like that." She pursed her lips. "I think you better do the fence first." She tapped one finger against her cheek. "Could you do the utility poles next and then the laundry room?"

"Sure, no problem. Whatever you want. I'm assuming the picnic areas will be last."

She smiled. "*Sí*, I think that makes the most sense. Finally, I'm seeing progress. I can't wait. As fast as you work, I'll—"

"Don't get your hopes up. The office is pretty simple compared to the outside. I might need to hire some day laborers to help me make the deadline."

"I know you can do it, *Manny*," she said, stressing his preferred name. She obviously knew what strings to pull. "I know you'll make the deadline and keep my Park open. But I realize it's a lot of work and if you need extra workers, you're the boss."

"Speaking of a lot of work." He strode to the windowsill and pulled a piece of rotten wood off. He held it up. "How did this place get into such a shambles?"

"I put off doing repairs trying to pay down my house mortgage, so I could use the proceeds to fix the Park up."

"Did you get it paid?"

"*Sí*, and the Park wasn't really that bad. Then we had a tropical storm last September. The wind and rain compounded the damage and destroyed some other stuff, like the utility poles and the fence outside."

"I see. No wonder I keep finding new things to fix. Like this window. It needs to be replaced."

She joined him at the window, fingering the rotten wood and the warped frame. "I didn't realize." She shook her head. "If it's more money you need..."

He hated it when she talked about money.

¡Maldita sea! Who was he fooling? He didn't care if she prattled about money all day. She was standing inches away, and he could feel her breath on his cheek. The vanilla smell of her swirled in his brain.

He didn't want to shut her up; he just wanted an excuse to kiss her. To cover her lips with his and take her breath into his body.

Leaning down, he brushed his lips against hers. Her hazel eyes went wide and then her eyelids drifted shut. He increased the pressure and tangled his fingers in her hair. She tasted as sweet as honey. Her lips were warm and firm and clung to his. Her mouth parted slightly.

He ran his tongue over her lips, seeking entrance. Widening the seam of her mouth, he thrust his tongue inside and tasted the hot essence of her.

Her eyes flew open, and her hands came up. She pulled free and pushed against his chest.

He got the message and let go.

She was panting, as if she couldn't drag enough air into her lungs. He understood how she felt. Then one hand flew to her mouth, and she frowned. "Who gave you permission to do that?"

"No one. I wanted to."

"You're not my boyfriend."

"I'd like to be."

"I don't want a boyfriend. And you can't work for me if you...if you..."

"Kiss you?"

"Yes." Balling her hands into fists, she backed away. "I hired you because I was desperate. And I didn't think you'd take advantage."

"Now wait a minute," he protested. "You kissed me back."

"No, I didn't," she lied and screwed up her face. "And I don't want...don't want...that. All I need are your carpenter skills. And I'm paying for your work. You're just a hired hand."

Just a hired hand.

The words reverberated in his brain. He'd never been so insulted in his life. He should have known better than to think she might welcome his kisses or anything else. Realizing how she felt, he didn't want to be around her.

"I need to get a new window and some Formica." He grimaced. "Don't worry, though, I'll be back to finish the office tomorrow. After that, I'll concentrate on the outside. You might start thinking about buying new washers and dryers. And you're going to need picnic tables and some kind of grills. Do you want me to tear down the old brick barbecue pits?"

"*Sí, por favor*, I think that would be a good idea."

"Consider it done. You know where to find me if you need me."

"Let me know if you have any questions or need other supplies."

"Sure."

He grabbed his toolbox and let himself out the front door. The bell tinkled overhead. Remembering how hopeful he'd been the first time he'd heard it, he wanted to yank the damned thing off and throw it into the Gulf.

Just a hired hand.

***

Catalina perched on the edge of the chair, feeling ill at ease. Glancing around *Señor* Galvez's office, she was impressed by the number of diplomas and certificates adorning his walls. He was obviously a good lawyer. And she was a charity case. He would know that, of course. How would he treat her?

She didn't have long to wait when Galvez breezed into the office, greeting her and introducing himself. Seated across from him, she had to admit Elena was right. He was handsome.

Almost too handsome. She found herself comparing him with Manny. Manny wasn't classically handsome, just masculine and rugged. Which was one of the reasons she was drawn to him. Handsome men put her off.

"May I see your papers, *Señora* Reyes?" Galvez interrupted her thoughts.

"Of course." She snapped open her purse, pulled out the documents, and handed them to him.

"Give me a minute to look them over."

"Sure. I really appreciate this." She folded her hands in her lap and tried to relax.

He smiled, but his smile couldn't compare to Manny's. Galvez only smiled with his mouth. When Manny smiled, his whole face lit up.

Why was she comparing the two men? She had no intention of dating either of them. In fact, she'd pushed Manny away when he'd kissed her and made it clear she didn't want him to try again. But he'd been right. She had responded to his kiss. They were attracted to each other. A sexual attraction.

That was why he was so dangerous.

She was glad he'd be working outside for the next couple of weeks. That way, they could both avoid temptation.

After what Nieto had done and then his unexpected death, she'd lost all feelings—at least the kind of feelings a woman had for the opposite sex. She'd been invited out by several men from her church, but she'd turned them down. She hadn't lied when she'd told Manny she didn't want a boyfriend. Maybe one day when she had the Park fixed up and her money problems resolved. Maybe then, she could let go of the deep-down hurt and betrayal she still carried in her heart. She was lonely, but she was also scared. She didn't want to get hurt again.

Manny Batista was different, though, and she could sense the raw magnetism between them. But she'd be a fool to fall into bed with a snowbird. What would happen when he left? She'd be even lonelier than she was now.

"*Señora* Reyes, *Señora* Reyes." Galvez broke into her thoughts.

"Uh, *sí?*" She licked her lips. "I'm sorry I wasn't paying—"

"That's all right." He smiled his fake smile again. His facial muscles barely moved. How did he do it?

"I've looked over your documents, and you did the right thing, comparing your property to other Parks in the area. This should be an open-and-shut case. I can file a tax appeal for you."

"And that should do it?"

"It should." He spread her documents on his desk and smoothed out the creases. "Except for one thing—your property fronts the ocean. Correct?"

"Yes, but—"

"That's why they raised your taxes." He cut her off again. She didn't like him interrupting her every time she opened her mouth. It was rude and smacked of arrogance, but then he was helping her for free, so she shouldn't complain.

"Beachfront property is very valuable," he went on, "but I'm sure you know that."

"But I'm not developing my property."

"That's what we'll explain to the County."

"Explain?"

"Yes, after I file the papers, there will be a hearing."

"I didn't know."

"Don't worry. I'll be right beside you."

She nodded, wishing she could force herself to say something nice, to show gratitude for his help. But he was too pretty-handsome, and he reeked of expensive cologne. Someone should tell him a little of that high-powered stuff went a long way.

Thinking about *Señor* Galvez dousing himself in pricey cologne, a giggle bubbled to her lips, but she bit her tongue and covered her mouth with her hand. He gazed at her, his eyebrows arched above his black-rimmed glasses.

She rose and extended her hand. "*Señor* Galvez, I can't thank you enough for your help. You'll let me know the date of the hearing?"

"Of course." He rose, too, and took her hand. His hands were smooth and soft as a baby's butt.

"Then I won't take any more of your valuable time. You have my phone number." She turned to go.

"Uh, *Señora* Reyes." She stopped and looked back. "Your friend, *Señora* Jiménez, mentioned you're a widow."

Here it came—the pitch.

Perdición take Elena!

She didn't want to go out with this oily attorney who doused himself in expensive cologne and who couldn't even smile properly. On the other hand, she didn't want to piss him off, either.

Gritting her teeth, she wished she could scream obscenities at the top of her lungs. This was what happened when you didn't have money—people took advantage of you in other ways.

"Yes, I'm a widow," she said.

"Would you like to go out?" he asked. "*Señora* Jiménez mentioned you were very attractive." He looked her up and down, like a butcher appraising a choice cut of meat. "But her description doesn't do you justice. You're a very lovely woman, *Señora* Reyes."

She bit her lip again. "*Gracias*, I appreciate the compliment. But about going out," she hesitated, forming an answer. "I'm in the middle of Park renovations that must be finished by the first of next month." She smiled tightly. "After the first of February... Well, you have my phone number."

"I'll make a note of it." He came around his desk and showed her out, placing his hand on her arm and giving it a gentle squeeze.

She shuddered and wanted to jerk her arm free. But she didn't.

***

Manuel eased himself into the leather recliner and clicked on the television remote. The TV set came on, voices blaring. He adjusted the volume. Not that he was going to watch anything; he just wanted some background noise while he rested his aching muscles.

He was accustomed to long hours and hard work, but the Park had just about bested him. He'd had to do a lot of heavy lifting, something he hadn't done in a long time.

He'd knocked out the office in a couple of days and started on the perimeter fence. With the help of a couple of day laborers, the job had gone quickly. They'd replaced the wooden-slat- and-wire fence in just three days. But the utility poles had been the worst. He'd dug out the old concrete bases and then poured new bases. He'd hired a day laborer to help him wrestle the heavy poles into place but even with help, the work had been a challenge.

Catalina had called the utility company to replace the wiring, so now she had more slots to rent. You would think she would have shown a little gratitude, but their exchange about the utilities had been brief and cold.

His stomach rumbled. He'd stopped mid-day and wolfed down a sandwich and a bag of chips. That had been hours ago. Now he was hungrier than a pack of teenagers raiding a refrigerator. But the thought of getting up and preparing dinner made him groan.

He could use a hot tub. Maybe he should move to one of the other Parks and soothe his aching muscles in their tub. But he was too exhausted to move. If he had half a brain, he'd throw in the towel and let Torres finish.

He'd wanted this job. Of course, at the time he hadn't known a simple kiss would send Catalina into orbit. But that was water under the bridge. He'd taken on the job, and he wasn't a quitter.

One good thing—he hadn't had time to be lonely. The backbreaking work had cured him. And lately, he'd been even more alone, too tired to visit with his neighbors.

His right leg went into spasm, the muscle drawing taut. He jumped up and walked off the cramp while reaching down to massage his knotted muscle.

Tomorrow, he'd push his sore muscles to the limit when he knocked down the old brick barbeque pits and finished patching the concrete floor in the laundry room. Luckily, there were only three barbeque pits, and the laundry room should go fast. After that, the hard labor would be done. All he'd need to finish was overseeing the placement of the new barbecue grills and tables, as well as the new washers and dryers for the laundry room.

Once the laundry room and picnic areas were complete, the remaining work would be Catalina's living quarters. And he doubted she would want him in her home. Besides, Torres was long past due to show up again.

Groaning, he settled into the chair and stretched his legs. His head lolled back against the soft leather. A short nap and then he would pick up some fast food.

Someone knocking on his trailer door jerked him awake. He cocked one eye open and wondered who it might be. Other than the Deckers, he really didn't know anyone at the Park, except to say hello. He went to the door and looked out the window. A stranger stood on his folding steps.

He opened the door to a tall, lanky man with graying hair. "Yes, can I help you?"

The stranger stretched out his hand. "Good evening, I'm Hank McCall." He pointed over his shoulder at space number fifty-eight, now occupied by a shiny fifth-wheeler Jayco. "Guess we're neighbors now."

Manny nodded. "Looks like we are. My name is Manuel Batista, but most folks call me Manny." He gazed past his visitor. "I like your rig."

"Yep, she's a honey, and this is our third year on the road. Never been this far south, though."

Manny chuckled. "Without going to the Florida Keys, I think South Padre is about as far as you can go." He stood to one side and opened the door wider. "Won't you come in?"

"Okay, but just for a minute. I didn't mean to bust in on you." He glanced around and his eyes widened. Like irate caterpillars, his thick, bristly eyebrows inched up his forehead, overshadowing his light blue eyes. "Say, you've done a lot with this old Airstream. She looks like new."

"Why, thank you. I'm a carpenter by trade. I enjoyed refitting her."

Hank shook his head. "I wouldn't even know where to start. I'm a retired software developer."

"That makes us about even. My son says I'm dangerous around computers."

"Sounds like a young 'un. My step-son thinks I live in an alternate universe." He chuckled. "I don't want to keep you, Manny, it being dinner time and all. But this is my first time here, and I drove up and down the road, looking for a grocery store or gas station, but I couldn't find anything."

"You came across the causeway from the mainland, right?"

"Yes, and I headed straight for the water. I drove up and down the beach, but this was the only RV Park with an ocean view. That's why I stopped here. I like being on the water. I'm from Lake Geneva in Wisconsin and—"

"Then we're twice neighbors." Manny slapped him on the back. "I'm from Chicago."

"You don't say. I lived in Rock Island until I retired a few years back."

"Can't blame you for retiring to Lake Geneva. It's beautiful. I used to take my family there for weekends to get away."

"Yes, it's pretty enough. But I got tired of all those long, cold winters."

"Me, too."

"You retired?"

"No, semi-retired, though my son would like for me to make it permanent."

Hank smiled and shook his head. "Kids, they think they own the world."

Manny laughed. He liked this guy, Hank. Seemed like a real down-to-earth person. He wondered if Hank's wife was as nice as her husband. "You're right, this *is* the only RV Park with ocean frontage."

"That's what I thought. And I noticed the renovations. I like that the owner is keeping up the place."

Manny's chest expanded. He wanted to tell Hank he was responsible for the renovations, but it would sound like bragging. If Hank stayed around long enough, he'd find out. "You said you need directions to a grocery store and gas station?"

"Yeah, if you don't mind. My cell is charging in the truck, or I wouldn't have to ask."

"Not a problem. I'm glad we got to meet." Manny paused. "When you came straight for the water and drove up and down, you were on Gulf Boulevard. That street is strictly for residences, motels, resorts, and RV Parks." He pointed over Hank's shoulder. "You need to go back down Boca Chica Road and past Gulf Boulevard to South Padre Boulevard and hang a right. South Padre is the main commercial street for the island. You'll find plenty of gas stations, convenience stores, and a couple of grocery stores, too. Just keep driving north."

"Hey, thanks. Are there cafes there, too?"

"Sure, lots of places to eat. *Louie's Backyard* has great seafood and nice views of *Laguna Madre*."

"That's the Bay I crossed over between here and the mainland?"

"Not a Bay, more like..." Manny shook his head. "Hard to explain, but Padre Island, which runs all the way to Houston, is like a barrier island. And in between Padre and the mainland is a body of water called the *Laguna Madre*."

"Yeah, now I remember from the maps. Pretty interesting. And this *Louie's* sounds good, too." Hank glanced around. "No missus or dinner cooking?"

Manny looked down at his feet. "Uh, no, I'm widowed."

"Hey, I'm alone, too. Divorced for a few years. I was in a relationship, but my retirement didn't sit well with my last girlfriend, so I'm tooling around on my own."

Manny raised his head. Hadn't Hank said it was "our" third trip? But they'd been talking about his rig. Maybe he meant him and his trailer?

"You want to catch a bite with me?" Hank asked. "You could show me around. Hell, I'll buy you dinner. It's the least I can do." Hank leaned against the open door. Manny couldn't be certain, but he thought there was a pleading look in the other man's eyes. He sensed his new neighbor was lonely. And he knew about loneliness.

Did he want to go to dinner with Hank?

Two old dudes going to dinner together? Not what he'd envisioned for himself.

He shrugged. "Sure, let's go."

***

Catalina stood to one side and let the delivery man pass, wheeling in one of the new dryers. She glanced around the laundry room. The foundation had been patched, and the laundry room sported a fresh coat of paint and new connections.

Manny had worked miracles with the Park in just a little over two weeks. She was ready for Fielder. She hadn't thought it possible in such a short time, but Manny had proven her wrong. He'd worked like a Trojan from sunup until past sunset. All the outside repairs were done.

"Put that dryer at the end." Manny's deep voice rumbled from the doorway.

Her skin tingled, and she wrapped her arms around her waist.

His bulky form filled the door, blocking the outside light. He'd taken off his shirt. A high front had moved in yesterday, bringing unseasonably warm weather for early February.

He nodded and strode past her, helping the deliveryman lift the dryer from the dolly. She couldn't take her eyes off him, couldn't drag her gaze from his naked chest. Without his shirt, his build was even more impressive than she'd imagined.

For a grandfather, he was hot. She shook her head. Forget the grandfather part. He was *muy caliente*, period.

Sweat glistened on his naked chest, tiny droplets of moisture clinging to the curling brown hair dusting his abdomen. His male nipples were large and brown. She wondered what it would feel like to lick them. She'd never done that, not even to her husband.

He might not have a six-pack, but he didn't have a middle-aged paunch, either. And his powerfully bulked pecs and work-hardened biceps were a sight to behold.

She licked her lips. Heat coiled through her, and her legs felt wobbly and weak. The old tension gathered at the base of her spine. She was aware of her erect nipples rubbing against the lace of her bra.

Even more, watching his straining, bulging muscles made her wet. Hot and wet and ready. She bit her lip, hoping the pain would force her thoughts back to the laundry room and away from the bedroom.

"*Señora* Reyes, *Señora* Reyes." A voice calling from outside penetrated her trance. Probably another delivery man. She left the laundry shed and walked into the bright sunshine.

Torres stood in front of his pickup truck, his arms folded. He was the last person she'd expected to see.

"*Buenas tardes, Señor* Torres," she said.

"What happened?" He unfolded his arms and pointed at the delivery truck.

"I found someone else to finish what you'd started."

"You can't do that." He spat on the ground.

"No? Why not?"

"Because we had an agreement. I had the job."

"But you left and I had a County deadline to meet. I couldn't wait."

He moved forward a step, his mouth pulled back in a snarl. "I told you I'd be back."

"Not soon enough, I'm afraid." If he thought he could intimidate her, he had another think coming.

She sensed Manny before she saw him. He'd come from the shed and stood behind her. She could feel the heat from his body and registered the salty, man-smell of him.

"*Señor* Torres, let me introduce myself." He stepped around her. "I'm Manuel Batista, and I'm a contractor from Chicago." He retrieved a white card from the pocket of his jeans. "Here's my business card."

Torres accepted the card and glanced at it. Then he looked at Manny, his gaze insolent but guarded. "So, what does this prove?"

"What *Señora* Reyes told you is true. She couldn't wait for you to come back. The County gave her a deadline and if she didn't meet it, she would have been fined and had her license revoked."

"She should have told me." Torres dropped his gaze and kicked at a rock.

Manny glanced at her.

"*Señor* Torres, I tried to tell you but you said—"

"Okay. Okay." Torres held up one hand. "I lost the job. You found another contractor because you had to." He shrugged. "I understand. You paid me for what I've done so we're square." He nodded at Manuel. "Nice to meet you, *Señor* Batista." He turned back to his pickup.

"*Esperáte*, wait," Manuel said.

Torres faced them again. His eyes were narrowed, and he frowned.

"The job isn't finished," Manuel told him. "I did the outside repairs to beat the County's deadline, but *Señora* Reyes' home still needs remodeling."

What was he doing, Catalina wondered? She didn't want Torres. Not after seeing the kind of work Manny did.

But could she be around Manny without jumping his bones?

Torres glanced at her. Manny turned his gaze on her. They were both waiting. The decision was hers.

"Is that right, *Señora* Reyes? You still have inside remodeling?" Torres asked.

She licked her lips and knotted her hands. Then she bit her lip again and chewed on it.

"Tell him," Manny urged.

Her gaze hooked with his and held. "I want you to finish my work, Manny."

Torres snorted and looked from Manny to her and back again. He kicked at another rock with his pointy-toed cowboy boot. "I guess that wraps it up. See you around."

She didn't pay attention as Torres revved up his pickup and drove away. All her attention was on Manny. He gazed at her for a long time, almost as if he could see straight through her, could read her mind and take her temperature with nothing more than his brown eyes.

"Do you mean it?" he asked. "What you told Torres."

She dropped her gaze and smiled. "I better. He's gone."

"That's not what I meant."

So he couldn't take a little teasing. "I want you to finish the job, Manny. You helped me when I needed you, and you've worked your butt off. I've never seen anyone work so hard. I couldn't have done it without you, and Torres couldn't have done it."

He nodded and crossed his arms over his naked chest. "I'm glad you're satisfied."

"I'm not just satisfied. I'm very happy." She smiled again and glanced at him. "And I can't wait until you remodel my kitchen."

"When do you want me to start?"

"How about tomorrow morning?"

"I'll be there at seven. That's not too early?"

"No, that's fine." He turned to go, but she put her hand on his arm. "And thanks for backing me with Torres. You didn't have to do that."

He stared at her hand, and she dropped it. "I wanted to help. He was being unreasonable." Manny strode to the laundry shed. "I've got to finish installing the washers and dryers. I'll see you in the morning." She watched as he disappeared into the utility room.

What had she done?

She'd sent Torres away and told Manny she wanted him to finish the job. Why had she done it? Out of gratitude? Or was she subconsciously plotting her own downfall? She could barely keep her hands off him now. What would happen, having him in her home day in and day out?

She liked and respected him and was impressed by his work ethic. On top of that, he was the only man she'd desired, other than her husband. She shook her head. Maybe she wasn't ready for an affair, but she liked having him around and a little flirtation couldn't hurt. Could it?

Maybe even a little kissing. She'd enjoyed his kiss, despite pushing him away. He had soft lips to match his soft brown eyes. Why not indulge herself? She was a big girl. She knew what she was doing. She'd keep it light, knowing he would be leaving in a couple of months.

Chapter Five

Manny arrived promptly at seven and pushed open the front door to the office. The bell tinkled, and this time it sounded friendly. Placing his toolbox on the counter, he glanced around the reception area and congratulated himself on how nice the new paneling, texturing and paint looked. Not to mention the mail slots and counter.

The rich aroma of coffee brewing tantalized his nose. He heard Catalina rummaging around in the back. He hoped she'd bring him some coffee.

As if his thoughts had conjured her, she appeared in the doorway with a steaming mug. "*Buenos días.*" She glanced at her wristwatch. "You're right on time." She smiled.

He liked it when she smiled. Her gray-green eyes sparkled. Today, she wore her russet-colored hair pulled back in a ponytail, but a few curling wisps had escaped, framing her face. If she looked this good in the morning with her face scrubbed clean, she must be a heart-stopper made up. Maybe he'd ask her out and see.

"*Buenos días,*" he replied.

"How about some coffee?"

"*Por favor*, if it isn't too much trouble."

"Of course not, how do you like your coffee?"

"Black with sugar."

She nodded. "I'll be right back."

He heard the clicking of toenails and *Migo* came hurtling into the office. Jumping up, the Lab put his paws on Manny's stomach and wagged his tail.

"Hi, boy." He scratched the Lab's ears and received a wet, doggy kiss for his efforts. He laughed and said, "Good, boy, good, *Migo*. I missed you too."

She returned with the coffee and handed him the mug. Grabbing her dog's collar, she said, "Come, *Migo*. Down, boy. Your new buddy and me have work to do. I'm going to put you in your run."

She left the room again, but his gaze went with her. She wore a high-necked, jersey pullover that on first glance appeared to be conservative. But the stretchy material hugged the full curves of her breasts, outlining their lush contours.

And her jeans were the usual faded denim, clinging in all the right places, so tight he'd almost swear she'd painted them on. Now, if she'd just bend over, he could...

"Where are you going to start?" He hadn't heard her return, lost in his horny fantasies.

"I thought you wanted your kitchen done first." He took a sip of coffee.

She rolled her eyes. "That's a wish come true. I can't wait. What part do you want to start on?"

"How busy are you? Can you help with the wallpaper? It would go faster with two pairs of hands."

She sucked her bottom lip into her mouth and nibbled on it. He watched, mesmerized. But that had gotten him into trouble before. He knew better. Dragging his gaze away, his eyes landed on the only discordant note in the remodeled office, the wilted plant by the window.

"Don't you ever water that thing?" he asked.

"What? Oh, you mean the dracaena?"

He pointed at the drooping plant. "Whatever it is, it looks like it could use some water."

"You're probably right. I always forget." She was off again like a bright hummingbird, flitting from flower to flower.

A few moments later she returned with a watering can and gave the plant a dousing. He ran his hand over the newly varnished counter and waited.

"Aren't you going to get started?" she asked.

"You didn't answer my question. Can you help out or are you too busy with the Park?"

"Sure, I can help if you show me how. Here, follow me." She disappeared into her living quarters. He followed her with his toolbox.

He finished his coffee and placed the mug on the kitchen counter. "Thanks for the coffee."

"Want more?"

"No, maybe later." He thrust his hands in his pockets and looked around. "Do you have wallpaper or paint picked out? What about the cabinets? Replace or refinish?"

She put down the coffeepot and glanced around. "I hadn't gotten that far." She laughed. "I was so worried about the Park, I didn't even think about what I wanted in here. Silly me."

"Time for you to do a little shopping. I can come back later." He grinned. "I've got a pile of laundry that I've been putting off—"

"But the stores aren't open yet."

"I hadn't thought of that." He felt foolish, forgetting how early it was. When he was around her, all rational thought flew out the window, and he existed solely on hormones.

"Have you had breakfast?"

"No."

"Want some? I was going to cook eggs and bacon. They say breakfast is the most important meal of the day."

"I've heard that, but I usually skip it."

"Not anymore," she said. "Not while you're working in my home. I'll be glad to cook for you."

"I can't put you to that much trouble."

What was she up to? Smiling, friendly and welcoming? This wasn't the Catalina he knew.

"It's no trouble. Have a seat. It'll just take a few minutes."

Thirty minutes later, he pushed back his plate and stretched his legs beneath her kitchen table. "That was great. *Gracias.*" He patted his full stomach. "Time for a nap."

She giggled. He enjoyed hearing her laugh. She sounded like a little girl when she giggled. "Does this mean if I feed you, you'll go to sleep?" She took his empty plate.

He sat up in the chair, pulling his legs in. "You know I wouldn't do that. I'll do my laundry while you decide what to get for your kitchen. As soon as you're back, we'll start."

Rising, his napkin slid to the floor. He'd forgotten about the darned thing. In his trailer, he used paper towels. Bending down to retrieve it, he knocked skulls with Catalina.

They both straightened, rubbing their heads and grimacing. Her mouth was only inches away. His gaze fixed on her coral-tinted lips, so full and inviting. He hovered over her, like an anxious bee over an exotic flower.

"I'm sorry," he said with a ragged breath. "I didn't know you would go for the napkin too."

She rubbed her forehead. "That's okay. No real damage done." He noticed her gaze was fixed on his mouth.

The temptation was strong, but he hesitated. He didn't want to ruin his long-range chances. *Go slow, muchacho, go slow.*

She licked her lips and closed her eyes. Thrusting her chin forward, she puckered up, waiting to be kissed. If that wasn't an invitation, he didn't know what was. And she looked like such a kid. Like she'd never been kissed before.

Oh, hell, he couldn't resist.

His lips brushed hers. Her arms came up and circled his neck. He deepened the kiss, pressing his lips against hers. She tangled her fingers in the hair brushing his collar. He licked her lips, slowly, sensuously, taking special care with the seam of her lips and the corners. She parted her lips. He slid his tongue inside and rubbed her tongue. She opened her mouth wider and twined her tongue with his.

Before he knew it, he was devouring her. His hand slid around her waist, and he pulled her closer. Her breasts flattened against his chest. He groaned into her mouth. Lower, his erection pushed against the denim of his jeans. Her hand drifted down the front of his shirt, caressing his chest. His cock was as hard as the utility poles he'd replaced.

He wanted nothing more than to strip her bare and take her on the kitchen floor. But he couldn't do that. He'd promised himself to go slow. True, she'd obviously wanted him to kiss her. But he didn't know if she was ready for more. Tentatively, he brought his hands up and under her breasts. His thumbs flicked over her hard nipples, budded beneath the clingy jersey material.

She moaned into his mouth and rubbed herself against his hands. Emboldened, he caressed her breasts, moving his fingers in slow arcs, pulling gently on her nipples. She wriggled in her chair, scooting closer, encouraging him.

Their hot kiss spiraled on and on. She'd unbuttoned the top two buttons of his shirt and smoothed her hands over his chest, her long, stiletto-sharp nails scoring him. But he didn't mind.

He'd bet she was a she-cat in bed. And por Dios, if he got any hotter for her, he'd explode.

Taking her cue, he bunched the bottom of her jersey top in one hand. His other hand traced the bumps of her spine. Slowly, softly, upward. Until he reached her bra. He'd undone a lot of bras in his time. With an expert touch, he unsnapped hers. The lush fullness of her breasts swung free. He reached his hands around and cupped her breasts, closing his eyes and savoring their satiny feel in his hands.

She stiffened and gasped.

Attuned to her, he lowered his hands. He broke their kiss and rested his forehead against hers. "*Lo siento.* I'm sorry. I shouldn't have—"

"It's okay. We both got carried away." She lifted her head and reached behind her back to clasp her bra. She avoided looking at him.

She'd stopped him again. Was she unsure of herself or of him? Probably the latter. Given his history with women, he couldn't blame her. But she didn't know that. Did she?

Feeling like an awkward teenager caught in the backseat of a car, he murmured, "I'll leave my toolbox. When you're done with shopping, come and get me. I'll be ready to start."

"Do you do floors?"

He crossed his legs and counted to ten. Good thing he'd been celibate for a long time. At least he'd had practice, forcing down his natural urges.

"Uh, sure, I do floors, if the tile pattern isn't too intricate."

She kept her eyes trained downward, as if she was studying her kitchen floor. But he had a feeling she was buying time, too.

"I saw some faux stone tile on sale. The squares are a good size. A simple pattern would be best." She bobbed her head. "You've saved me a bundle, Manny. I think I can splurge a little. Can we gut the kitchen and start over? Cabinets, floor, a new sink, paint, and wallpaper. I might even be able to get granite for the counters if I can find a deal."

"Ask for a remnant from another job—that's how to get a deal on granite."

"Thanks, I'll do that." She lifted her head and glanced at him. But then she looked away quickly. "A whole new kitchen. I'm so excited!"

Not as excited as he was. But at least his erection was subsiding.

"*Bueno.* I'm glad you're excited, but you need to go shopping first." He shook his head. "You're the only woman I know who has to be told to go shopping."

She giggled again—that little-girl giggle. She was such a study in contrasts—a low throaty speaking voice mixed with a high-pitched giggle. An angry, cursing witch—a soft-as-butter kisser. A tough-as-nails businesswoman—a self-conscious girl when it came to her sexual needs.

He'd love to peel back all her multi-layers and find the real Catalina.

But would she let him? And should he get involved, knowing the vow he'd made when he'd lost Lydia?

***

Catalina proudly showed Mr. Fielder around the Park, pointing out the renovations. Fielder trailed her with his clipboard, checking off the list. She'd been outside walking *Migo* when he'd driven up.

Because she'd met Fielder outside, he hadn't seen the office yet. She was saving it for last. She loved her new office—it was like a different room with its gleaming counter, new paneling, and a fresh coat of paint. Not to mention the rebuilt mail slots and a new window.

Manny had even thrown away her bedraggled dracaena when she wasn't looking and presented her with a beautiful, leafy ficus tree. If she could just remember to water it.

Then he'd brought her a new table and chairs. She'd protested his extravagance, telling him to take them back. He'd explained he couldn't because they were from the local traders' market.

She'd given in and paid for them. They hadn't cost much. As a final touch, she'd spread current issues of *Motor Home* and *RV Magazine* on the table. Now she had a real office, an office she could be proud of.

Fielder pinched his nose and made that peculiar honking sound she remembered. Did the man have allergies or just terminal sinuses?

"Have you seen enough? I'd like to show you my office."

"That's fine." He made another check mark and stowed his pencil.

She opened the door and stood to one side. The angry hum of a buzz saw told her Manny was hard at work in the kitchen.

The balding bureaucrat glanced around her office and made a semi-grunt of acknowledgement. Was it a sound of approval or disapproval? Who could tell? For all she knew, he was clearing his sinuses again.

He paced the length of the office, peering into corners and at her new plant. He went behind the counter and ran his hand along its Formica top. And he studied the mail slots for a moment.

"Very nice," he said. "Quite a change."

Furious hammering sounded in the back, almost drowning out his words.

"Thank you," she said.

"Having more work done?" He hitched one shoulder in the general direction.

"Yes, my living quarters are in the back." And if he thought she was going to show him her private space, he better think again. The County had no right to tell her how to live. Only how she ran her Park.

"Anything more you need to see?" she asked.

"No, I think that will do it."

Relief washed over her. The muscles in her shoulders loosened and the knot in her stomach eased. "So, the Park passes inspection."

"Not quite." He raised one hand and beckoned. "Follow me outside, please."

Wariness replaced relief. *What now?*

They walked to the south end of the Park where there were several vacant spaces. Retrieving his pencil, he used it as a pointer, ticking off space eighty-seven, eighty-eight, and ninety. "See those cracked slabs, Mrs. Reyes?"

"Yes." She closed her eyes, afraid of what was coming next.

"They'll have to be replaced."

"Why? Cracked slabs weren't on the list. And besides—"

"They weren't on the list because there were so many other violations that—"

"What about the slabs that are rented out? Do you want me to crawl under people's motor coaches looking for cracks?" she asked.

He shot her a warning look.

She subsided, waiting for the inevitable. What she wouldn't do to have a good scream and let off some steam with a few choice words.

"I wouldn't go looking under rented spaces, if I were you," he said. "You don't want to upset your renters. South Padre and Brownsville relies on winter Texans for a large part of their annual revenue. We must make every attempt to accommodate these folks and maintain high standards. Otherwise, they'll go somewhere else to spend their money."

"Of course, I understand." But she didn't. A cracked slab wasn't exactly life threatening. Why did she have the feeling someone at the County had her singled out?

"I'm glad you understand our position." He handed her a piece of paper.

She glanced at it. The paper contained a rough drawing of the Park with certain spaces noted. Counting them, she groaned under her breath.

"I've marked down the ones with cracked slabs," he said. "You'll need to replace them."

"I see." He'd indicated sixteen spaces. She hated to think how much it would cost. And she'd splurged on redoing her kitchen. "How long do I have?"

"How about another thirty days?" The edges of his mouth quirked into the semblance of a smile. "I think that should be plenty of time."

"Yes, plenty."

"Other than that, Mrs. Reyes, everything looks fine. I'm glad you cleared up the violations."

"Yes, thank you."

A blanket of dullness settled over her, blocking out the urgency of the situation. She felt hemmed in and surrounded, struggling against a huge, formless mass she couldn't get a grip on.

But she forced herself to go through the motions, seeing him to his car, accepting the new license he'd granted, and watching him drive away. She gave a little wave as his car pulled onto Boca Chica Road, and then her legs crumpled and she sank to the ground.

If she weren't outside in the open before God and everybody, she'd burst into tears. And there was no place to hide. Manny was inside.

Manuel...she'd have to ask him about the slabs. And she'd have to go to the bank and take out a loan. She'd exhausted most of her cash reserves and had hoped the inside work would be finished before her money ran out.

She hated going into debt again, but she didn't have a choice. Not if she wanted to keep the Park.

***

Manny leaned over the new counter, watching Catalina through the office window. Why was she sitting in the dirt?

He'd known the County inspector was going over the Park because he'd overheard them. He'd expected Catalina to run back inside, happy and relieved. After all, he'd finished everything on the list. And he was damned proud of his work. Even Catalina had said the Park had never looked better. So what was the problem?

His first inclination was to go to her, but he squelched that particular urge and watched to see what she'd do. After their hot-as-pepper kiss in the kitchen, she'd kept her distance and been cool toward him. Nice, but distant.

Whatever was wrong, he'd find out soon enough. One way or the other. There was work to be done. He headed back to the kitchen.

A few minutes later, the door between the office and kitchen swung open. Manny glanced up to find Catalina standing in the doorway, looking like an orphaned kitten who had been kicked.

Again, he told himself it wasn't any of his business, but the message didn't make it from his brain to his mouth because he found himself asking, "What's wrong, Catalina?"

"Oh, it's...nothing." She crossed to the sink and started stacking dishes in the new cupboard.

"I've about got the hard stuff done in here," he said, hoping to cheer her up. "Have you decided on the paint and wallpaper yet? I know you were down to a couple of choices."

Turning from the sink, she glanced around the room. But the look in her eyes was flat, the spark in their depths extinguished.

She gazed at him. "You've done a great job." But her praise was as flat as the look in her eyes. "Why don't you take the afternoon off? I think I've decided on the paint and wallpaper. But I need to run to the store to get them."

"You should also think about what you want to do with your living room."

She turned to look at the corner that served as her living area. Anchored by a moth-eaten area rug, her sitting room consisted of a beat-up sofa and a ragged recliner, along with a dented coffee table and an ancient console TV with rabbit ears.

"I don't think there's anything you can do, Manny. I need to find some new furniture."

"What about a little paint or new paper above the wainscoting?"

"Maybe." She cocked her head and considered. "I'll think about it while I'm looking for the kitchen."

"You really want me to knock off for the rest of the day?"

"Yes, but come back for supper around seven. Okay?"

An invitation to dinner—he was speechless. She'd kept her promise and fed him breakfast and lunch when he would let her, but he'd never been invited into her sanctuary after dark. Was this their first date?

"Can I bring anything?" he asked.

"I was going to grill some *fajitas*. But I don't have any liquor." She glanced at him. "What do you drink?"

"Beer goes good with *fajitas*."

"Sounds good. Bring enough for me."

"Sure."

He gathered his tools and put them in his toolbox. Then he put the guard on his circular saw and hoisted it to his shoulder. "See you at seven."

She nodded and started stacking dishes again.

He didn't want to go. He gazed at her back, trying to understand. She was wearing a T-shirt that stopped at the waist of her jeans, displaying the flare of her hips and the rounded moons of her perfect tush.

Just looking at her got him all hot and bothered.

But that wasn't the feeling overwhelming him as he gazed at her slender back. He wanted to comfort and protect her. Take her in his arms and shelter her from the world. Soothe away the disappointment in the depths of her eyes. Make her sparkle again, as only she could sparkle.

Maybe she'd tell him what was wrong tonight and accept his comfort. He hoped so, because as he turned to go he had the strangest feeling she was trying not to burst into tears.

***

Catalina checked the flank steak sizzling on the grill and then hurried into the kitchen to cut up the lettuce, tomatoes, and onions. *Migo* shadowed her, wagging his tail. He was in his customary begging mode when she grilled meat, hoping for scraps.

She shredded the lettuce and chopped tomatoes. When she started dicing the onions, her eyes burned and teared. She swiped at them with the back of her hand. After this afternoon, she would have sworn she didn't have a drop of moisture left in her body.

Glancing at the clock over the sink, she saw it was almost seven. She didn't want Manny to see her crying, even if it was only from the onions. Earlier, she'd fought to hold onto her self-control until he'd left. But he'd known she was upset.

She didn't know what had prompted her to ask him to dinner. Probably because she was feeling vulnerable after Fielder left. Without Manny renovating the Park, she'd be in deep trouble. And she needed his advice about the slabs. She'd come to rely on him, and she trusted him, too. He'd worked so hard, and she knew it wasn't about the money. She could tell by his hesitation when she paid him.

He wasn't just a hired hand. She could bite her tongue in two for having called him that. She'd considered apologizing but the time hadn't been right. And then he'd kissed her again, so it didn't matter. And this time, when she let him know they'd gone too far, he'd stopped. He'd been the perfect gentleman. Even though it was pretty obvious they were both hot for each other.

Manny was her friend.

She wanted him as a lover but after what had happened with Nieto and knowing Manny would be leaving in a couple of months, she didn't think she could go down that path. But she did want his friendship—it was the reason for her dinner invitation. She wanted to know more about him. What he thought and felt about things, not just how skilled he was with his hands or how strong his back was.

Thinking about his body, electricity ran down her spine and she shuddered, going hot and then cold.

Could they be friends? Or were they destined to be something more?

She'd left the door to the office ajar so she could hear the bell. But when it tinkled, announcing Manny, she jumped and almost sliced her finger off.

She put the knife down and wiped her hands on a kitchen towel. Nervous, she smoothed the front creases of her slacks. Manny hadn't seen her in anything but jeans, so she'd dressed for dinner. She'd worn her nicest pair of dark green slacks and a matching sweater.

"May I come in?" His voice rumbled from the doorway.

She turned to face him. "Please do."

He stood in the door, holding a brown grocery bag.

Migo sprinted over and threw himself against Manny's chest, barking and twisting the back part of his body in doggie ecstasy. Manny laughed and patted his head, getting a drooling kiss on his hand.

"Down, *Migo*. Down, boy." She grabbed the Lab's collar and pulled him off. "Can I take your bag?"

He laughed again. "I think you have your hands full." He pulled out a longneck Lone Star beer. "I'll just put these in the fridge."

Letting *Migo* go, she turned to Manny. "Are you going to share?"

"Of course. I hope a twelve-pack will do."

"That should be more than enough." She pushed the hair from her face and smelled meat burning. She rushed to the back door. "Oh, my gosh, I forgot the steak."

Outside she grabbed the tongs and quickly shoveled the blackening meat onto a platter. The back door opened and slammed. Manny had followed her. She didn't want him to know she'd ruined dinner. She was usually a good cook, and she'd wanted everything to be perfect.

He came up behind her, cupping her shoulders in his big, warm hands. Then he gave her a gentle squeeze. "You don't know it, but I like my meat charred. My family thinks I'm crazy, but my mother wasn't much of a cook. She usually got caught up with us kids and forgot about what was on the stove. I learned to like burnt food if I wanted to survive."

She turned around and gazed at him. "You're just saying that so I won't feel bad."

He raised his right hand, palm out. "Scout's honor. I know you're a good cook, Catalina. You've been feeding me for the past few weeks. And I'm not lying about my mother."

"What did your wife think about burned food?"

He frowned and broke eye contact. "Lydia didn't mind. She'd cook stuff for the kids and feed them while she let mine burn."

"You're kidding."

"Nope. She was an understanding wife."

"When did she die?" She asked and then bit her lip. "I'm sorry, what I meant to say was how long have you been a widower?"

He stepped back. "Are you sure you want to hear about it? How about a beer first? Do you want one, too?"

"*Sí*, I want a beer." She grabbed the platter and handed it to him. "But I don't like burned *arroz y frijoles*. I need to get back inside."

He laughed and gave her a mock bow. "Your wish is my command, Red."

She stopped and turned with her hands on her hips. "What did you just call me?"

"Red."

"I thought you agreed not to call me that."

He stroked his chin. "You're right, I did, and a promise is a promise." His brown eyes lit up, and he grinned. "Can I call you Cat?"

She frowned and sniffed. "Well, I guess that's okay. Anything but Red." Then she remembered the food in the kitchen and turned around, rushing to the stove.

Pulling the lids off the rice and beans, she found she'd returned in time. She turned off the gas jets and carried the pots to the table. Then she retrieved the lettuce, tomatoes, and onions from the butcher block, along with the *pico de gallo* from the fridge. Now all they needed were tortillas.

Manny came into the kitchen and opened the refrigerator, pulling out two beers. He opened them and joined her at the table.

"Looks great." He took a swig of beer and handed her the other bottle.

"Corn or flour?" She took a sip of beer and grimaced at the bitter, yeasty taste. She wasn't much of a drinker, but tonight she wouldn't mind getting a little drunk.

"I like corn best."

"My favorite too." She popped a stack of corn tortillas into the microwave. "The joys of modern technology," she quipped, taking another sip of the beer. The beer wasn't so bad, once you got used to it.

The microwave timer dinged, and she put her beer on the counter. Concerned the burned meat was getting cold, she jerked open the door and grabbed for the plate. Pain lanced through her hand, and she jumped back, dropping the tortillas and clutching her burned hand. The plate shattered, spilling bright orange tortillas over the floor.

"*Maldita...*" She clenched her jaw shut.

Manny took her hand in his. Turning it over, he leaned down, gently blowing on her stinging skin. Then he lowered his head and kissed her palm, salving her hurt with his soft, full lips.

Closing her eyes, she leaned against the counter, her body melting. She savored the sensation of his mouth on her hand and she wanted more. Wanted his lips on hers and his big rough hands on her heavy, aching breasts.

The phone rang, breaking her trance. She opened her eyes and blinked, realizing what had been about to happen. Was she ready? The phone shrilled again, pulling her back to reality.

Murmuring a quick apology, she pulled her hand free and crossed the room, reaching for the wall phone.

Chapter Six

Manny walked to the back door and went outside. He stared at the dying embers in the grill and downed a second beer. He wanted a third, but not enough to go back in and listen to Catalina's one-sided conversation.

The caller was a man. He had no doubt of it. Her home afforded no privacy unless she went into the bathroom, and the cord from the wall wasn't that long. Cat was the only person he knew who didn't own a cell phone.

Por Dios, he hadn't wanted to listen, but he couldn't help it. At first, the conversation had been about business—something about a hearing for property taxes. He'd expected her to hang up after that. But then he'd realized she was making excuses for not going out. Not wanting to hear the outcome, he took another beer from the fridge and went outside.

Migo nosed open the back door and pawed at his trousers. Leaning down, he stroked the Lab's soft fur. "How about a run, old boy?"

Taking *Migo* by the collar, he pulled open the wire gate to the dog's run and put him inside. The Lab turned and barked, lifting his muzzle to the moon and proclaiming his loneliness.

Manny could sympathize with his four-footed friend.

A shaft of light pierced the darkness. Turning, he saw Catalina's curvaceous form in the doorway. "I'm sorry for the interruption. Let me heat up the meat and tortillas. Okay?"

He opened his mouth to ask about her injured hand. Then he closed it. What did it matter? Why should he care? She had other boyfriends.

Other boyfriends.

Snorting, he gave himself a dose of reality. He wasn't her boyfriend, only a hired hand. And tonight was an aberration. The County inspector had upset her today, and she'd turned to him. Probably because there was more work to be done.

That was it. She'd invited him to dinner to soften him up. To ask him to do more work. Not because she wanted to spend time with him. Why hadn't he thought of it before?

"Manny, are you all right? I'm going to heat up dinner. Okay?"

"Sure, great, go for it."

"Don't you want to come inside?"

"I put *Migo* in his run. Is that okay?"

"Of course. But come inside." She wrapped her arms around her waist, pushing up her full breasts. "It's getting chilly out."

"In a minute."

"Fine. Dinner will be ready." She closed the door, cutting off the shaft of light, leaving him in darkness.

He stared at the star-sprinkled sky, gathering the chilly air into his lungs. She was right. The weather was turning cold. The first cold weather he'd experienced in the Valley. It reminded him of home and his kids.

What was he doing here?

Busting his hump for a woman who obviously had mixed feelings about getting intimate. He'd never encountered that problem before. Before, the women had come to him, and he'd taken what they offered. He hadn't pursued a woman since he was a teenager.

He shook his head. Should he bother to stay for dinner or should he leave and cut his losses? He'd do her damned work anyway. She didn't need to soften him. Shaking his head again, he pushed open the back door and stepped into the blinding light.

Catalina glanced up from putting bowls on the table to find Manny standing there. He was frowning and that wasn't like him, usually he was easygoing.

"Have a seat," she said. "Everything's on the table. Can I get you another beer?"

He set his empty down. "I better slow down. Are you going to have another?"

"No." She surprised herself. She'd thought she wanted to get drunk but after grappling with Galvez on the phone, she'd changed her mind.

"How's your hand?" he asked.

She glanced down. The skin was red and it ached dully. She'd forgotten about her hand and what Manny had done. Remembering, she trembled and an electrical tingle streaked through her, pebbling her nipples.

"The hand's fine." She held it up and wriggled her fingers.

"Do you have some aloe?"

"Yes, in the medicine cabinet."

Nodding, he strode to the bathroom and pulled open the mirrored cabinet door. Funny, she didn't mind him going through her things. Watching him, her gaze skimmed over his broad shoulders and flat abdomen.

He'd dressed for tonight too. He wore a deep burgundy chambray shirt, setting off his dark coloring, along with well-pressed khaki pants that displayed the powerful muscles of his thighs.

As he rummaged through the medicine cabinet, she didn't know if she wanted him to find the cream. If he touched her again, she'd melt in his arms.

"If you can't find it, don't worry. I'm fine. Dinner's getting cold…again."

He held up a tube and grinned. Returning with the aloe, he handed her the tube. "Better put some on."

He wasn't going to touch her. She slumped and a strange mixture of relief and regret sluiced through her. She took the tube and spread the aloe on her hand.

"Okay?" she asked. "Why don't you sit down?"
"I'd like a glass of water. Can I get you one?"
"Sure."
He crossed to the sink and filled two glasses. "Ice?"
"No thanks."
He returned with the glasses and set them on the table. Then he circled behind her. She tensed, wondering what he meant to do. Then she heard a scraping sound. Glancing back, she realized he was holding the chair for her.

Touched by his gesture, she said, "*Gracias.*"

"*De nada.*" He rounded the table and took his seat.

Silent minutes ticked by as they passed dishes back and forth and heaped their plates with food. After cleaning his plate, Manny said, "Great *fajitas*. My mother couldn't have done better."

"I'm glad you liked them."

He pushed his plate to one side and placed his elbows on the table. "Hadn't you better tell me what's going on?" He'd rolled the sleeves of his shirt to his elbows, uncovering his muscular forearms.

Gazing at the potent male strength of him, she longed to run her fingertips over his arms and chest, memorizing the corded feel of his muscles.

Flushing hot, she grabbed her glass and took a cool drink of water. "What are you talking about? Nothing's wrong."

She'd wanted them to have a pleasant evening, to talk about their kids and get to know each other. But the night was already ruined. First, by what had happened today and then by the phone call from Galvez. And she suspected Manny was jealous because another man had called her. Not that he had the right to be.

They were friends—not lovers—if only she could convince her body.

He took a sip of water. Gazing at her over the rim of the glass, he said, "Cat, you can't fool me. I want to know what upset you this afternoon. And if it isn't too personal, I'd like to know about the phone call. What's going on with the Park? After all the work and time I've spent on the place, I think I have a right to know."

She swallowed a forkful of rice and nodded.

"And I need to know something else."

"What's that?"

"Why this Park has such a hold on you."

She lifted her head and met his gaze. "I don't know what you mean."

"I think you do. This place means more to you than just a living."

Was she that obvious? She gazed at his face and lost herself in the depths of his cocoa-colored eyes. He would understand if she told him.

"You're right, Manny. The Park isn't just a living. It's my dream. And I sacrificed a lot to have it."

"Go on," he said.

"When my children were little, I worked night jobs as a waitress so Nieto, my husband, could stay with the kids. He was a mechanic and worked during the day. About fifteen years ago, I saw an advertisement for a receptionist and clerk for the Park. The hours varied, sometimes during the day, sometimes the evening. By then my kids were older, so it wasn't a problem. Just a longer commute than I was used to. We lived in Brownsville."

"You started as an employee here?"

"*Sí*, for an older widowed lady, Yolanda Zamora. She had no family and needed help."

"It's a long way from being an employee to owning a Park with an ocean view."

Her brow pleated and her mouth turned down. She lowered her eyes. "*Sí*, a long way. I fell in love with the place," she almost whispered and lifted her head. "Mostly the sea. Though I'd lived in Brownsville all my life, I hadn't come to the ocean much. We brought the kids here on weekends to play on the beach. But when I came to work here and saw the Gulf every day—somehow, I knew this was where I belonged."

"So you and your husband bought the place? On your salaries as a waitress and a mechanic?" He sounded skeptical.

She flushed, realizing how crazy it sounded. "It wasn't that easy."

He took a sip of water. "I'm not surprised."

"I became good friends with the owner, Yolanda. She had no one. She was widowed. She and her husband had had only one daughter, who died young in a car accident—"

"My wife died in a car accident."

"Oh, I'm sorry. I didn't know."

"It's okay. Go on."

"Well, after I'd worked here for a couple of years, Yolanda came to rely on me, more and more." She looked down and felt the heat rush to her cheeks. "Yolanda told me I reminded her of her daughter."

"That's understandable, given the circumstances."

She glanced up. "*Sí*, it was." She hesitated, folding and unfolding her napkin. "Most of Yolanda's family had either passed on or lived far away in California or the East Coast. This land was hers from a Spanish grant to her family going back to the eighteenth century."

He whistled long and low. "Interesting, about the history of the place." Leaning back, he crossed his arms on his chest.

"The longer I worked here, the frailer Yolanda got. I became more of a nurse than anything. She relied on me for everything. There were weeks when I only got home for a day or two."

"I'm surprised she didn't sell the place and move to a retirement home."

"You mean a nursing home. She thought about it, but she loved the ocean, and she wanted to die here. It was all she really had."

"I bet she got lots of offers for the land."

"*Sí*, some very lucrative ones. Several consortiums wanted to put high-rise condominiums here. But she was old-fashioned, and she didn't want the land developed."

"And an RV Park is about as natural a setting as you can have, while still earning a living. Right?"

"Yes, that was the way she felt. When I'd been here almost nine years, she passed away in her sleep, the day after she turned ninety. I threw a big party for her birthday. Everyone came, Nieto and my kids and all the renters." She knotted her hands in her lap. "When her will was read, much to my surprise, she'd left me the place—but with one stipulation. In my lifetime, I couldn't develop the land. I must keep it as an RV Park."

"What about selling the land? Forgive me for prying, but it's a fascinating story. Did she put any stipulations on how long you had to keep the place?" He uncrossed his arms.

"No, she didn't." She shrugged. "I guess Yolanda knew me better than I thought. She must have known I would move heaven and earth to hang onto it. And I did have to take over her mortgage. She still owed money from when she and her husband had developed the Park."

"So, you stayed here, slaving away, to keep it." He tugged on his earlobe.

Her gaze followed his gesture. What would his earlobe taste like if she nibbled on it? Male. Pure male. Even though he'd dressed up, he hadn't doused himself in cologne. He smelled like soap and starch, but mostly man.

"*Sí*, it was such an incredible opportunity, to own a place like this. For me, paying off a modest mortgage was nothing, compared to what she gave me. I wanted Nieto to quit his job and help me run the Park." She bit her lip and lowered her head. "I hadn't been home much for the last couple of years, trying to take care of Yolanda. And I thought Nieto understood..."

"But your husband didn't understand?"

She shook her head. "No, he didn't. Said our family had already sacrificed enough—that he couldn't tell me not to take care of Yolanda because it had been the right thing to do, but once she was gone he wanted nothing to do with the place. He wanted me to sell it and use the money for our kids' college. Otherwise, they'd need to scramble for scholarships and grants and take out loans. On our salaries, we hadn't been able to save much. I tried to convince him if the Park was properly run we'd make plenty of money for the kids' college." She shrugged. "But he didn't want any part of it, wanted me to shut the place down, come home and concentrate on our family. Alba, my oldest, had one more year of high school. It was true I'd been gone a lot and..."

"What did you do?"

"I stayed here and ran the Park. I still went home, but it wasn't the same. It was as if..." She stopped herself. She couldn't tell Manny what her husband had done when she'd refused to sell.

"You know, it's hard to blame the way your husband felt. If you'd barely been home for several years, I can see—"

"Don't even go there." He'd lulled her into a false sense of security. For some reason, she'd thought he would understand. But he didn't. He was being as negative as everyone else. First her husband, then her kids, and now the County. The one person she'd thought would understand—didn't. Despite all his hard work to restore the Park.

She rose and gathered the dinner plates. Her initial hurt coalesced into something darker and stronger. Her stomach churned and her ears burned. Who did he think he was, passing judgment on her dream?

"I think you should go, Manuel. You asked, but you really didn't want to hear what the Park means to me."

He moved behind her at the sink and grasped her shoulders, pulling her around. "I'm sorry. That wasn't right—I shouldn't have passed judgment on what you decided." He sighed, breathing into her hair. "I guess I felt for your husband. If you were my wife and you wanted to stay away from me, I would..."

The touch of his callused hands on her arms burned through the fabric of her sweater. She could feel her heart pounding in her chest. Could he hear it? Was his heart pounding too? Did he know how he made her feel? As if she was climbing the walls.

Should she forgive him for taking her husband's side?

Moments before, she'd been as mad as a displaced hornet. But when he touched her, she couldn't think straight. All the anger drained from her body, leaving only the ache of desire behind.

She gazed into his soft, brown eyes. His black pupils were dilated. His hands on her arms trembled. He desired her too.

She pulled free and moved back a step. What had he said about "if he were her husband?" She didn't want to go there. Instead, she asked, "Haven't you ever had a dream?"

Needing to keep busy, she went back to the table and gathered the glasses and silverware. But he was still standing at the sink, barring her way.

"Yes, I've had dreams." His voice sounded ragged. "I wanted my own contracting business. I wanted my children to grow into responsible adults." He pulled his hand through his hair. "I even dreamed of returning to the Valley and staying the winter."

"So they all came true."

"Yes, but there was a price."

"Your wife, Lydia?"

He nodded.

She put the silverware and glasses on the counter. "I lost Nieto, too. We were separated, but I refused to give him a divorce, thinking he would come around." She shook her head. "But I lost him anyway. And I hadn't seen him much those last few years, so..."

"You felt guilty, on top of everything else."

She nodded and blinked back tears. She thrust her chin out. She usually didn't cry. What was happening to her? She'd suddenly turned into a watering spout.

"What happened to your husband?" His voice was gentle.

"Undiagnosed high blood pressure. Nieto hated doctors. He had a heart attack and was gone." She snapped her fingers. "Just like that." She couldn't tell him the rest, what she'd learned before he'd died. The real reason Nieto had wanted a divorce.

"How long ago?"

"A little over three years. I'd just paid off the mortgage here. Thought I would hire an assistant and have more time with him but..."

"It must have been hard. What about your kids? How did they take it?"

"Oh, they came around, mostly. They'd stayed with Nieto because their school was in Brownsville and all their friends. Alba had gone off to design school and was in her last year of a three-year program. Carlos was halfway through college." She paused and pushed back her hair. "I think they've finally forgiven me for being away so much. At least, my son Carlos has. Alba, is another story." She shook her head. "I tried to see them as much as I could, but I couldn't afford an assistant, and all my extra money went toward helping them with college. Luckily, they were smart, and they both got scholarships and grants to help." She raised her head and gazed into his eyes. "Nieto and I couldn't afford big insurance policies. When he died, there was just enough for his final expenses and to help Carlos finish school. Our home was mortgaged, and I had to pay it off before I could remodel the Park. I finally paid off the mortgage and sold our home. But it was a modest house, so I had to be careful with the money."

"You told me that's why you didn't make repairs."

"That's right, and the tropical storm last autumn didn't help." She shrugged. "Now I've got to go into debt again. When I thought I was free."

"The inspector found something today?"

"*Sí.*" She licked her lips. "Sixteen cracked slabs, to be exact."

"That's a lot of concrete work."

"You can't do it? But you set the utility poles."

"Minor stuff." He shook his head. "For sixteen slabs, you'll need a mixer. I'll have to rent one. And it will take several men to break up the old slabs and get the new concrete poured and leveled."

"You're right. I didn't think."

"You should find a contractor who specializes in concrete work. Do you know of anyone?"

"Torres?"

He shook his head again. "Torres is a handyman. He'd sub the job to a concrete guy and it would cost you extra." Pausing, Manny considered. "Let me do a little online searching. Do you have a computer? I'll see what I can find."

"Would you? My good friend, Elena, showed me how to get on my computer, but I haven't used it again, and I don't know how to look up stuff. Elena showed me how to research my property taxes, but I don't know if—"

"No worries. Just point me to your computer and put in your password. I'll Google local concrete sub-contractors. Then I'll visit with a couple and get estimates. I think I have a pretty good idea what a fair price might be, though, it's probably cheaper here than in Chicago."

Nodding, she sprinted up the stairs and came back, lugging a soft computer case. She plugged in the computer and typed in the password she'd memorized. She pulled out the chair for him.

"I can't thank you enough, Manny. I don't know what I'd do without you."

Nodding, his gaze fixed on her face—or more accurately, on her mouth. She knew what he was thinking because she was thinking it too. And this time, she wanted him to kiss her—and not just because she was grateful, either. She wanted his mouth on hers, commanding her senses and body, taking her to a place where only a man and a woman could go.

He dropped his eyes and squatted in front of the computer. She leaned forward and touched his arm. Slowly, he raised his head. Their gazes locked and held. He got to his feet. And this time she didn't close her eyes. This time she wanted to experience his kiss with all her senses.

As if it were the most natural thing in the world, his mouth descended on hers. His lips were full and warm and moist. Soft, too, and giving. He tasted of onions and grilled meat, but she didn't mind. She liked onions and steak.

His lips moved over hers, and he explored her mouth, finding different angles to kiss her, bringing their lips together in a variety of ways. His tongue brushed over her bottom lip before he thrust it inside.

She kissed him back with all her long-suppressed need. Lacing her arms behind his back, she held on. He reached down and snapped the computer shut with one hand. It closed with a loud click, making them both jump and pull back.

They laughed, their breaths commingling. And then his mouth covered hers again. He nibbled the corners of her lips and brushed his tongue inside. When her tongue met his, a jolt of electricity shot through her. She held him tighter, clinging to him while her body melted in his embrace.

With his strong hands at her waist, he guided her toward the couch, his mouth never leaving hers. Eagerly, she followed, her body humming with desire, dazed with longing. Her breasts felt hot and heavy, straining against her bra, begging to be touched. And lower, the old, familiar tension gathered at her spine.

He pulled her down on the couch. She expected his hands to start exploring her body like the last time, but he surprised her. He kept kissing her with the same intensity, as if her mouth was the only thing in the world. And it needed to be properly cherished.

Sinking lower in his embrace, she concentrated her energy on kissing him back, on exploring every crevice and curve of his lips. He responded with even more passion, kissing her harder, taking as well as giving.

Then he murmured something and lifted his mouth from hers, trailing tiny kisses across her chin and down her neck. Behind her ear, his lips tickled her sensitive skin and made her gasp. His hand came up and covered her breast.

He pulled away and gazed into her eyes, as if silently asking permission. The weight of his hand on her aching breast felt so good. She didn't want to pull back this time. Didn't want him to stop.

She covered his hand with her own. He pressed down and lowered his head, trailing fiery kisses up and down her neck. His hand moved in a gentle, caressing motion over her breast. Cupping her fullness and then sliding up to tantalize her nipple, drawing it into a tight, hard point through the fabric of her bra and sweater.

She gloried in him touching her, and she lifted her arms and laced them behind his neck, combing her fingers through his straight, brown hair. His mouth trailed down her chest, kissing both her breasts through the wooly sweater.

Her clothing was becoming an encumbrance, an irritating barrier. As if he could read her thoughts, he lifted the bottom of her sweater and placed his hand inside. Slowly, he explored her stomach and then caressed her breast. His fingers worked their magic, rubbing the lacy material over her sensitive flesh. The friction against her nipple was pure, sweet agony.

She arched into his touch and pulled his shirt from the belt of his pants. Even dressed up, he didn't wear an undershirt. Her nails scored his back, branding him as hers.

Madre de Dios, how she wanted this man!

His large, rough hand covered her breast and then some. What would it feel like to have him on top and straining inside of her? Was he as big down there as…? As if in answer to her question, she felt the length of him against her abdomen.

Was she ready for this…ready to take a lover?

She'd never slept with anyone but her husband; and it had been a long time since they'd been intimate. If she wasn't ready, she never would be. He was a stranger. But a trusted stranger, someone she could count on. Her thoughts played Ping-Pong in her head, pulling her first one way and then the other.

Manny lowered his hand, pulling it free of her sweater. Smoothing the wooly cloth over her breasts, he lifted his head and kissed her thoroughly. This time, he didn't try to unsnap her bra. Instead, he reached down and cupped her woman's mound in the palm of his big hand. Applying pressure, his fingers caressed her clitoris through the fabric of her slacks and panties.

She lifted her hips off the couch, grinding herself into his hand. He pushed down harder and the pressure built and built. Within a few seconds, she groaned, "*Madre de Dios*. Oh, Manny." And then she splintered into a thousand tiny pieces; the ecstasy sweeping her along and her vagina muscles contracting.

Panting, she turned her face into his neck and held tightly to his shoulders. Slowly, she floated back to earth and looked up at him. Their gazes caught and snagged. She'd thought she was cooling off but gazing at him, she could feel her body flush with heat.

He'd just brought her to orgasm with a few seconds of pressure—she hadn't realized how needy she was. And thank the Lord he hadn't said anything.

He lowered his head and started to nuzzle her breasts. They were both fully clothed. But he must have had other ideas because the next thing she knew, he'd unzipped her slacks and had his hand down the front of her panties.

She'd known what she was getting herself into—hadn't she? After all, he'd made her come. She should return the favor—shouldn't she? But heavy petting was one thing; going all the way, quite another. *Madre de Dios*, she sounded like a horny but conflicted teenager.

Trying to ignore what his fingers were doing down there and how wet she was, she slid her hand down the front of his pants and cupped his erection through the fabric of his khaki pants.

Emboldened, he took the waistband of her slacks and pulled on them, trying to slide them down her legs. She tried to relax, really tried, but knowing he intended on undressing her and taking her on the couch, her body stiffened.

He must have felt the change in her because he lifted his mouth and let go of her slacks. He glanced at her and nodded. Then he pulled her slacks back up and zipped them.

As if nothing had happened, he said, "I think I could use another beer." But the look in his eyes said something totally different—that he understood.

She wasn't ready to take him as a lover, and he understood. Would she ever be ready?

Or would she live alone in the Park, struggling to make ends meet until she was too old to fight anymore? Too old to care?

Manuel Batista hadn't promised her anything except to help get her Park remodeled. And in a few weeks, he'd be leaving. He'd happened to be here when she needed him. That was all—she shouldn't give herself to him out of gratitude. But as soon as the thought entered her head, she dismissed it.

She wanted him. But if she slept with him and he left, how would she feel?

"Earth to Catalina," he teased gently, rearranging his large frame on the couch. Scooting to the end of the sofa, he leaned against the arm and crossed his legs.

She straightened her clothes and smoothed back her hair. "I heard you. You'd like another beer. So would I." She smiled and couldn't help but tease. "You know where the fridge is."

He started to rise, but she laid one hand on his shoulder. "I was kidding...kidding. Stay put. I enjoy waiting on you."

His gaze met hers, probing, searching, asking. She knew what he wanted. Would their relationship grow and deepen? When would she be ready? She shook her head. She was too confused and uncertain.

"I'll get the beers," she said.

He dipped his head. "*Bueno.*"

Rising, she got the two beers from the refrigerator and opened them. Then she noticed the *flan* sitting on the back of the shelf. "I forgot. I have *flan* for dessert. Do you want some?"

He chuckled. "Not with beer. But don't throw it out. I'll eat the *flan* tomorrow."

His simple words arrowed straight through her heart. Nieto used to talk like that. Used to save his dessert for the next day. She and her husband had had a lot of good years together before things had fallen apart. The cozy domesticity of her relationship with Manny left her aching for more.

Did she want to spend the rest of her life with Manny?

But it wasn't meant to be. He hadn't spoken of love or marriage or any of those things. Their attraction was simple lust—animal magnetism. Is that all she wanted?

"Hey, where did you go to get those beers?" He turned on the couch and glanced over his shoulder.

"Keep your shirt on." Then she realized what she'd said and blushed. She'd been the one taking his shirt off a few minutes ago.

Where did they go from here?

Chapter Seven

Manny watched as Catalina sauntered across the room, a beer in each hand. He must be nuts. Certifiable. Ready for the looney bin.

She'd wanted him as much as he wanted her. After touching her and bringing her release, how could he go back? Her flesh had imprinted him, left an indelible mark. Her breasts were soft and warm and round. Heaven on earth. And her mouth was enough to drive him berserk with desire.

Sure, she'd been a little scared, a little hesitant. What decent woman wouldn't be? Not that he knew much about decent women, except for Lydia. Cat hadn't told him to stop, though he'd sensed the change in her body.

But that should have been his cue to press harder, cover her with kisses and drive her as wild as she drove him. He should have unhooked her bra and suckled her breast, continued to play with her clit, knowing how needy she was, how hot and wet she was.

Then she would have been his.
Down, muchacho, down, give yourself time to cool off.

He didn't know when something inside of him had shifted, but she meant more to him than casual sex. And he'd given up casual sex when he'd tried to save his marriage. Unfortunately, he didn't live in South Texas and couldn't offer her a relationship.

He wanted her and he believed she wanted him, too. But after she came, she'd pulled back, retreated. Something wasn't right. Something had stopped her. Some doubts or fears. And he was doing his best to respect her feelings.

The question was—could he keep his hands off her?

Joining him on the couch, she handed him a beer.

"*Gracias.*" He tipped back the long-necked bottle and took a deep swallow. "Where did we leave off?"

"You were going to find a contractor for the concrete work."

"Oh, yeah." He waved his hand in the general direction of her computer. "I'll do that first thing tomorrow. How long do we have?"

"Thirty days."

"Plenty of time. All we have to do is find the right guy at the right price and get on his schedule."

"In the meantime, I need to go to the bank and take out a loan."

"I'm sorry, Catalina."

He was beginning to understand how she hated to be in debt. He set his bottle on the coffee table and took her hand in his. He wanted to offer her money. Give her an interest-free loan. He could afford it. But something held him back.

When it came to money, she was touchy and unpredictable. There was no telling how she'd react. His safest course of action was to say nothing and let her get the money at the bank.

"I appreciate your concern, but I'll be fine," she said, pulling her hand free. "My bank knows I'm a good risk."

Frowning, he rested his hands on his thighs, wondering why she didn't want to hold hands. What was she afraid of? Taking another swig of beer, he wanted to ask about her caller, but she surprised him by bringing it up.

"You asked about the phone call. It was from an attorney who's helping me with my tax situation."

"What tax situation?"

"The County quadrupled my property taxes at the beginning of the year." She shook her head and sipped her beer. "If I were a suspicious person, I'd think they were out to get me."

"Any reason they should be?"

"Maybe one, but I don't like to think about it."

He raised his eyebrows. "What happened?"

"I had a really good offer from some developers last autumn. They want to buy my land and build high-priced condominiums. I turned them down." She thrust out her chin and took another sip of beer.

He was beginning to understand her body language. When she fussed with her hair, she was gathering her thoughts. When she nibbled her lip, she was nervous or anxious. And when she thrust out her chin—that was her stubborn look.

His gaze dropped to her full lips. He'd like to nibble her lips. She had a great mouth. Perfect for kissing.

"Manny, did you hear what I said?" She interrupted his runaway thoughts.

"That you want to keep the Park."

She shot him a look from beneath her long eyelashes. "I wasn't sure you were listening."

"I was listening," he told her half of the truth. "With the County inspector on your heels and your taxes quadrupling, you think someone's trying to drive you out."

"I don't want to think like that, but sometimes I can't help myself." Folding her arms, she scooted forward to the edge of the couch. "Especially after today. Those slabs aren't critical."

"You never know, though, the inspector could just be overzealous." He paused for a moment, considering. "Corruption on the county level." He set his beer down again. "It's not uncommon. I've seen it happen in Chicago."

"What should I do?"

"What does your attorney say?"

"I haven't told him my suspicions. He filed a tax appeal and there will be a hearing."

"Let me ask you something. Have the developers been back?"

"No."

"Then it's probably not collusion. Probably just an unfortunate sequence of events." He retrieved his beer and downed the last of it. "If the developers come back, knowing you're facing financial difficulties, then there might be something. In any case, you should mention it to your attorney. Prepare him." He turned his gaze on her, wanting to judge her reaction, wondering what this lawyer meant to her.

"I guess I'll do that. And wait and see." She fiddled with her beer bottle, scraping at the label with her fingernail. Glancing at his empty, she asked, "Want another?"

"Sure." He really didn't, but he didn't want the evening to end, either.

Rising, she crossed to the fridge again. His gaze followed her, particularly the sway of her hips. He wanted to pursue this attorney thing, but he bided his time, wondering how to broach the subject without sounding jealous.

She handed him the beer. He took it, thinking this was his limit. Glancing at his wristwatch, he realized how late it was.

"I'm going to let *Migo* in," she said.

"That's a good idea."

Waiting on the couch, he chewed on his thumbnail. How could he find out about the other guy without prying?

Migo bounded into the room, wagging his tail. Jumping onto Manny's lap, the Lab put his paws on Manny's shoulders and licked his face. Manny laughed and scratched his ears.

"Come on, *Migo*, come down from there." Catalina grabbed the dog's collar and shooed him to his bed in the corner. "Time for bed, *Migo*."

The Lab whined and tucked his tail but did as he was told, shuffling to his doggie bed and flopping down.

Catalina paced for a moment in front of the coffee table and then sat across from Manny in the recliner. She grabbed her beer and scraped at the label again.

Manny knew it was late. Was she giving him a signal? He didn't want to wear out his welcome, but he had to know about the attorney before he left for the night. If he didn't find out, he wouldn't sleep.

"Uh, Catalina, I don't want pry into your, er, personal affairs. But I thought you were short on money. Aren't attorneys expensive?"

"*Sí*, that's what I told Elena."

He frowned. "Who's Elena?"

"Remember, Elena, my good friend."

"Oh, yeah, the friend who helped you with the computer."

"*Sí.*" She smoothed back her hair.

Dios, but he loved her hair. Long and curly with fiery red highlights. He fantasized about how she would look, like Lady Godiva, wearing just her hair and nothing else.

"Elena and her husband own a string of auto repair shops and *Señor* Galvez is on retainer, so they offered—"

"To let him help with your property taxes." That surprised him. Catalina wasn't the charity type. Elena must be a very good friend.

"I told Elena I'd only accept if the case didn't take too much of his time."

Swallowing his beer, he thought about what she'd said. Still no hint at what he'd overheard. The guy wasn't just an attorney, and he wasn't just doing a favor for Catalina's friend. *Señor* Galvez was after more than that.

He rose. "*Señor* Galvez sounded like a close friend, too."

Catalina stared at him, and her eyes narrowed. She pursed her lips.

He'd overstepped his boundaries, but damn it, how else could he know? Not that it was any of his business. They weren't really dating, and he didn't have any ties on her.

Fisting his hands, he told himself to butt out. As usual, his body didn't follow what his mind suggested. Thinking about Galvez kissing Catalina and touching her soft round breasts, a rush of adrenaline poured through him.

Fight or flight.

He clenched his jaw. *Por Dios*, he was ready to fight. Spoiling for a fight. The green-eyed monster had its claws in him and was taking him for a ride. And if he saw this Galvez guy sniffing around, he would…he would… He loosed his hands and told himself to stop. He couldn't do anything because he didn't have the right. Catalina wasn't his.

"Manny Batista, if I didn't know better, I'd say you were jealous." She rose, too, and faced him. The top of her head came mid-way up his chest. "And you shouldn't be. We're not even dating."

"I told myself the same thing."

She shrugged. "Then what do you care?"

"You know I care," he shot back, too quickly.

"Really? What does that mean?"

He broke eye contact and lowered his head. He stuffed his hands in his pockets. "You want me to spell it out for you?"

"*Por favor.*"

"I'd like for us to date."

"You haven't asked me."

"I'm not sure where I stand with you. A hired hand and all that…"

"You don't let things go—do you? I thought tonight was—"

Catalina and the Winter Texan

"Good for you, maybe." He ran his hand through his hair. "Damned frustrating for me."

"Oh, so that's how it is?" She grimaced and her eyes flashed emerald sparks. "Wanting to make me feel guilty and beholding?"

He felt the back of his neck heating. He looked away. "Forgive me. I shouldn't have said that."

She blushed, too. "No, you shouldn't have. I thought you were more of a gentleman."

He spread his hands, palms out. "Believe me, I respect you, Cat. When it comes to...comes to..." He cleared his throat. "I hope you *wanted* me to kiss you, not because you feel grateful for what I've done around the Park."

She shook her head. "So you've said before. And men say women don't make any sense," she muttered. "I wanted you to kiss me and more, Manny. It's just that—"

"And I want you, too, Cat. I want to spend time with you and not just working around the Park together. I've..." He shook his head. "Damn, this is hard to talk about." Then he lifted his head and caught her gaze. "I want us to go out, to dinner and a movie maybe. Or you could come to my trailer and I'll cook for you."

"What if I want to go out with Galvez, too? Does dating you mean we're going steady?" He heard the taunting tone in her voice.

He shrugged, thinking their discussion was going no place, except to get them both angry. But he was already in too deep. If he didn't say what he was thinking, he'd burst.

"Do you even like this Galvez—or are you going out with him because he's helping you? Is it the same with me? I'm fixing up the Park, so you invite me to dinner. But you won't commit to dating. I don't understand."

She stared at him, her eyes stone cold. "Galvez lives in Brownsville, at least. You live in Chicago. You say you want to go out, spend time with me. But where are we going with this? You want a relationship but on your terms. Have a vacation fling and then go back to Chicago." She bit her lip. "I don't know if I can do that. Nieto and I were high school sweethearts and then we married. I don't have much experience at dating."

"You mean since you lost your husband, you haven't—"

"No, I haven't dated anyone. A few men from my church have asked." She lifted one shoulder and let it drop. "I guess they didn't interest me or I wasn't ready."

He raised his eyebrows and shook his head. She really was an innocent. No wonder she'd been so reluctant to kiss him and more...

His heart plummeted. So his suspicions were correct. She wanted a relationship. It was all she'd known, married life to one man. He couldn't blame her for leading a sheltered life. And he didn't want just a quickie fling, either. He'd sworn off casual sex forever...or so he hoped. But a long-distance relationship—that was another kettle of fish. Most of them didn't work out, besides being damned frustrating.

"You're right." He reached out his hand to her and then let it slowly drop to his side. "I can't offer you a relationship. I'll be leaving in a few weeks, but I..." His words trailed off. There was nothing left to say, was there?

Her eyes looked suspiciously bright, as they had this afternoon when Fielder left. She turned and crossed to the sink. "Please go now, Manny. I'm tired and it's late."

"I'll go, but I'll be back tomorrow after I talk to some concrete people," he said.

"Don't bother. I'll find—"

"Oh, no, you won't. I know how you feel right now. But this isn't about us. This is about finishing your Park, and I'd like to see it through." He glanced around. "And *por favor*, I want to finish your home, too. I want you to have a nice place to live." He hesitated and cleared his throat. "Let me do the work for you—I want to. It means a lot to me."

She stood bent over the sink, rinsing off the dishes. She didn't turn and look at him. He could barely make out the words when she said, "Thank you, Manny, that's very kind of you. Have a good night."

***

Catalina pretended to be making herself a sandwich. But it was a cover for watching Manny painting the trim in her kitchen. After the trim, he'd hang the wallpaper. She'd probably have to help him. When it came to wallpaper, two sets of hands were better than one.

That should be interesting, she thought, slapping a piece of ham on a slice of bread. Interesting to hang wallpaper with someone you were trying to politely avoid. They'd reached a civilized arrangement. He would finish the work in her home, and he'd already found a concrete contractor for the slabs.

But no matter how civilized they were being on the outside. On the inside, she ached for him. Yearned for the feel of his strong arms around her and trembled with wanting him to kiss her again. He'd been honest, at least, he would leave in a few weeks and that would be that. Why did the only man she'd wanted since Nieto have to live hundreds of miles away?

Hazards of running an RV Park, she guessed, though she'd never been tempted before.

She'd called Elena and cried on her best friend's shoulder. Elena had done her best to soothe her and told her to take advantage of Manny's willingness to help. But Elena didn't understand how she felt about Manny. Instead, Elena had urged her to go out with Galvez.

Catalina snorted. That was the last thing she wanted. Galvez was fine as an attorney but nothing else. And she'd already turned him down twice. She hoped he would take the hint, and she prayed he wouldn't hold it against her. She needed him for the tax hearing.

"Would you like a sandwich, Manny?"

He glanced up, carefully holding the dripping brush in his big hands. Hands that had gently cradled and caressed her breasts.

"No, thanks, I'm going to knock off early if that's okay with you. My neighbor, Hank, wants to see some of Brownsville. We'll probably get a bite to eat, too."

She wondered what "guy" things they were going to do in Brownsville. Probably find a bar and look for women who didn't mind a little casual sex. She prayed they wouldn't bring the women back to the Park, but of course they had every right to.

Thinking about it, her eyes burned and she sniffed. She had to stop thinking about Manny that way. It was none of her concern. And maybe she was being too hard on him; maybe he wasn't that kind of man.

Besides, they'd come to an understanding—a civilized understanding. But *Madre de Dios*, why did it have to hurt so much? Like losing Nieto all over again.

"Not going to start the wallpaper today?" she asked.

"Nope, and it will have to wait. The concrete guy is coming tomorrow. I expect a full day, getting the slabs poured."

"Oh, I'm glad you told me because, I won't be around the day after tomorrow. I have my tax hearing." She managed a thin smile. "I'd planned on giving you the day off."

"Sounds good. Tomorrow will be a long day. The concrete mixer will be here as soon as the sun is up." He wiped his paintbrush on a ragged piece of cloth, dipped the brush into turpentine, and then wiped it again.

She watched him. His movements were slow and deliberate. As if he had all the time in the world. As if he didn't want to go.

All it would take was one word from her, and he'd stay. She knew it—knew the power she had over him. Just like the power he held over her. *Perdición*, this was pure torture. Being around him and not being able to touch him.

He raised his head and gazed at her. She could read the yearning in his brown, soulful eyes, but there was no help for it.

Trying to keep her tone casual, she said, "I hope you and Hank have a nice time in Brownsville."

***

Manny sat outside his trailer fiddling with a piece of driftwood, waiting for Hank. This particular piece of wood was almost as broad as it was long. Running his hands over the gnarls and knotholes, he let his thoughts wander and take flight. He pictured a nativity scene in his head and knew he had his subject.

Satisfied, he began to make a few careful cuts, roughly notching the outline into the wood. He heard a low rumble and glanced up, looking out to sea. A storm was gathering over the ocean, but it was miles away. If rain was coming, the sooner the better—before they started pouring concrete.

Thinking about the concrete—and, by extension, Catalina—his hand slipped and he cut his finger. Damn! He had to stop thinking about her. He stuck his injured finger in his mouth and sucked on it. The wound wasn't deep, only a surface cut. But he needed a bandage. He rose and reached for the door handle to his trailer. He glanced at Boca Chica Road.

Where was Hank? He'd quit at Catalina's home early to meet him, but his neighbor wasn't back from fishing yet. Then he heard a car approaching. Turning, he saw Hank pull up in his pickup truck. His neighbor waved and pulled the truck over to the side of the road.

Manny waved back and went into his trailer to get a bandage.

When he came out, Hank was waiting for him.

"Sorry I'm late, but the grouper were running. I caught a string of them. We'll have to fry them up. I put them in my freezer for now."

"Sounds like good eating. I was wondering what was keeping you. It's getting late to see the sights of Brownsville."

"Not for what I have in mind. I'll drive. You ready?"

"Sure, let me lock my trailer."

Manny opened the passenger door and got into the pickup cab. How pathetic was this, a boy's night out. Hell, he'd only agreed to go with Hank after Catalina had told him she didn't want to date. And his neighbor was always asking him to do something. Hank was the sociable sort. It was obvious he didn't like doing things by himself.

"Where did you say we're going? I thought you just wanted to look around town."

"You'll see." Hank winked broadly.

Manny didn't like the sound of that, but he was already committed.

They crossed the causeway and drove to the center of Brownsville but when they stopped in front of a neat brick building on Main Street, Manny's jaw dropped. Hank had brought him to a seniors' recreational hall.

He turned and glared at Hank.

Hank's grin was sheepish. "Hey, don't knock it until you try it. Maybe we'll meet some nice people."

Sure, Manny wanted to say, *and maybe a blue norther will coat Brownsville in a blanket of snow*. But he couldn't get the words out. He gritted his teeth and shook his head.

True, he was middle-aged, but he was a long way from the bingo-playing, square-dancing senior set. Or so he liked to think.

Briefly, he considered leaving Hank and calling a taxi to take him back to the Park. But he'd be damned if he'd pay through the nose to be driven all the way to South Padre. No, he'd tough it out, but this was the last time he'd accept an invitation from Hank. If his neighbor was lonesome, it wasn't his problem.

Reluctantly, he trailed Hank into the recreational hall. Entering the foyer of the cavernous room, he glanced around. Hank had obviously planned when would be the best night to come. Paper streamers and balloons festooned the room. On a raised dais at the end of the hall, a six-piece orchestra played. Couples whirled by, locked in each other's arms.

At least they were playing big-band tunes from the forties. He could handle that a lot better than square dancing. They stopped at a registration table in the foyer, and Hank must have sensed how displeased he was because he paid both of their entrance fees. A silver-haired, birdlike lady greeted them warmly and introduced herself as Mrs. Sylvester.

Hank introduced them. Manny smiled thinly and nodded.

Uncertain of what to do next, he stood with Hank on the threshold, surveying the scene. How many times had Hank mentioned he'd been married—two or three times? Obviously, his neighbor was no amateur at finding women. Based on a quick scan of the room, Manny would bet there were about three women to each man. And that wasn't counting the blue-haired ones over seventy.

He spied a long, tablecloth-draped refreshment table. He'd worked through lunch and turned down Catalina's offer of a sandwich. His stomach growled and rumbled. According to Mrs. Sylvester, their entrance fee included refreshments. He'd thought they'd go to dinner, and he was more than hungry. Without a word to Hank, he crossed to the table and looked over the spread. Not a real dinner—munchies mostly, but he'd make do.

Taking a paper plate, he loaded it down with sausage rolls, cheese and crackers, various dips and chips, and pizza slices. A real junk food fiesta. He bit into a sausage roll. Not wanting to appear too conspicuous by hanging around the food, he noticed a bulletin board behind the table. A calendar of events was tacked to the board.

With goodies in hand, he moved to the board and scanned the calendar. A fishing competition, bingo games, quilting and square dancing, not to mention bridge parties were scheduled for the upcoming weeks. Unfortunately, those activities left him cold—even the fishing. He'd tried his hand at fishing but hadn't caught anything.

He started to turn away when he noticed an arts and crafts show the day after tomorrow. Seeing the notice, he wanted to sign up and bring his carvings. He'd never shown them to anyone before except family. He had no idea what strangers would think of his sculptures, but the artist in him wanted to find out. At least if he attended the show, this ridiculous evening wouldn't be a total waste.

Someone tapped his shoulder, and he turned around.

A plump, nice-looking woman with blonde streaks in her brown hair gazed up at him.

"Can I help you?" he asked.

She offered her hand. "I'm Esmeralda Garcia. I thought you might like to dance."

He gazed across the room. The ratio of women to men hadn't gotten any better. He shouldn't be surprised he'd been tagged. But he didn't want to dance. Hell, he didn't even want to be here. But how could he refuse without hurting her feelings.

Nodding, he said, "My name's Manuel Batista. Glad to make your acquaintance, Esmeralda." He held up his plate. "I apologize, but I haven't eaten all day. Just let me finish and I'll come and find you—"

"Ah, Manny, here you are. I wondered where you'd wandered off to." Hank materialized at his side.

Sensing his reprieve was at hand; Manny turned to Hank and said, "This is Esmeralda Garcia. Esmeralda, let me introduce my friend and neighbor, Hank McCall."

Hank took Esmeralda's hand and kissed it. "Pleased to make your acquaintance, Esmeralda."

Manny almost choked on a cracker.

Esmeralda lit up like a Christmas tree and giggled. "Happy to meet you, sir."

"Would you like to dance?" Hank asked.

Esmeralda darted a quick glance at Manny. He'd just taken a bite of pepperoni pizza.

"Uh, *sí*, I mean, yes, I would love to dance." She lifted her head. "I just adore Glenn Miller, don't you? Though, he was a little bit before my time." She giggled again and laced her arm through Hank's. "My friends call me Esme."

They joined the other couples on the dance floor.

Manny polished off his plate and turned back to the notice for the arts and crafts fair. Less than two days, he wondered if it was too late to sign up. Should he go back to Mrs. Sylvester and ask?

A tall, Nordic-looking blonde woman approached him. He cringed inwardly, expecting another dance invitation.

"Hello, I'm LuAnn Sparks, the activities director." She looked him up and down, and then offered her hand. "You're new. I haven't seen you before. Down for the winter?"

He took her hand and shook it. She had an amazing grip. "Yes, I'm here for a few weeks." He inclined his head toward the dance floor where Hank and Esmeralda were energetically fox-trotting. "My friend brought me tonight. This is my first time here." He placed his empty plate on a side table.

"I take it you don't like to dance."

"No, I dance some. Not much of a fox trotter, though."

"I thought not. There are so few men, it's tricky to say no when you're asked to dance. But your friend rescued you and Esme seems happy."

Whew, this was one perceptive woman. Good looking and with a great figure but not his type. Though there'd been a time when all women were his type. Not now. Catalina's gray-green eyes and fiery red hair haunted him. He didn't want to dance with or touch any other woman. If only he'd felt this way when he'd been married to Lydia.

"I see you're interested in our activities. If not dancing, what are your hobbies? As the activities director, I always like to know what new people want."

"Oh, I'm interested in the arts and crafts fair. But it might be too late—"

"Not to attend, of course. You want a booth? It is a bit late, though allowances can always be made. What kind of craft would you like to exhibit?"

"I make wood carvings."

"Oh, how marvelous. A sculptor. I can't wait to see your work. Though, officially, we aren't taking any more exhibitors, but—"

"I understand. That's all right. It was just a spur-of-the-moment thing."

She winked at him. "Ah, but it helps when you know people in high places."

He didn't know what she was getting at. "I guess you're right."

The band's rendition of Glenn Miller's *Little Brown Jug* ended. Hank and Esme drifted to the other side of the hall, laughing and talking. Maybe Hank wouldn't be lonely anymore. Manny hoped so.

Esme looked young to be here—much younger than Hank. Which made him wonder about LuAnn's age.

He scrutinized her face and came up blank. She was attractive with bright blue eyes and a turned-up nose. And she could be any age between forty and sixty. Well-preserved and attractive, that summed up LuAnn Sparks.

Several frowning women watched them, shooting envious glances. He felt like the tables had been turned, and suddenly, he was meat on the hoof. And LuAnn certainly knew what she was doing. She'd claimed him as her own in this female-dominated world, and she wasn't letting go. He had to give her credit for her initiative and tenacity.

She led him back to the registration desk. "Manuel? Can I call you that?"

"Sure, LuAnn." He grinned.

"Manuel, I want you to meet Mrs. Agnes Sylvester, my right hand." She indicated the silver-haired lady who'd signed him in. "Agnes, this is Manuel, he's new to our center. And we're lucky to have him, I might add. He's polite, well-spoken, and a sculptor."

"Mrs. Sylvester and I met when we came in." This time, he offered his hand.

She took his hand and gave it a firm shake. "Agnes," she corrected.

"Agnes then."

An awkward silence followed as if LuAnn expected him to make small talk. When he didn't speak, the two women began a spirited but hushed conversation. Even though he was standing close, he had to strain to hear their words.

He'd been surprised LuAnn had introduced him to another woman, as possessive as she appeared to be. But of course, Agnes was well over sixty, and he doubted LuAnn perceived her as a threat.

Age was so important at this type of gathering. Thinking about it depressed him. Now he knew why he could have throttled Hank for bringing him. It wasn't because he didn't like the activities. The artificiality and posturing of the people left him cold. But he'd made up his mind to show his work at the fair.

"Could I sign up for the arts and crafts fair?" He interrupted the hushed discussion between the two women.

LuAnn turned to him. "Of course, I'm sorry. Agnes and I got carried away with the arrangements. We're in charge and other people don't always fulfill their obligations."

"That's too bad," he said.

"Yes, it is," LuAnn agreed and Agnes nodded.

LuAnn turned to Agnes. "Please, could I have the signup sheet for the fair?" Then she faced Manny. "There's a small entry fee, to cover expenses."

"How much?"

"Ten dollars." LuAnn handed the sheet to Manny.

He scanned the contents, mildly surprised to see around fifty signatures. Must be a lot of artists in the area.

"Ten dollars, that's a bargain." He signed the sheet and reached for his wallet.

Agnes, the keeper of the cash box, took the bill from him and gave him a receipt with a booth number.

"Where will the fair be?" he asked.

"Across the street in our picnic area," LuAnn said.

He couldn't wait. He'd never done anything like this before. Offer his art for sale. Just thinking about it made him excited. And if he could wish for anything more; he'd wish Catalina would happen by and see his sculptures.

But he realized how unlikely it was. She had her tax hearing that day.

Why couldn't he stop thinking about her?

Chapter Eight

Catalina stood in front of the Tax Review Board, her hands knotted together. She'd explained her position and Galvez had entered the tax assessments for the other RV Parks into evidence. When she'd faltered, he'd taken up the slack and stepped in, clarifying certain points.

She glanced at him and smiled wanly, wondering what came next. He returned her smile and held his right thumb up, indicating he thought the hearing had gone in her favor. She hoped he was right. If she won today, she was definitely in his debt. He'd been more than helpful.

But she didn't want to be in his debt. As nice as he'd been, she had no intention of going out with him. She wanted Manny, not Galvez. But that wasn't meant to be.

Thinking about Manny and how he'd kissed and caressed her made her cheeks burn.

Staring at the State of Texas seal behind the long table where the review board sat, she didn't realize the hearing had been recessed until the board members started filing out and Galvez raised his voice to a loud whisper, telling her it was over.

Her shoulders slumped, and she felt like a punctured balloon. It was such a relief to know her part was over. Now all she had to do was wait for the board's decision.

Turning around, she faced Galvez across the gleaming oak table. He smiled again and told her she'd done great. She thanked him and said she couldn't have done it without him. He grinned like the cat that had swallowed the canary. Unfortunately, she knew who the canary was.

"How about lunch?" he asked.

"What about the hearing?"

"The board is taking a break for lunch." He rose and came around the table. "They'll hear a couple more cases after the break and then render their decisions. We've got plenty of time."

"Okay. When should we be back?"

"Not until around two."

"I don't know," she evaded. "You must have other clients who need—"

"I left today open because I didn't know what order they'd take us in."

"All right, let's go to lunch, but it's my treat. Please." If she paid for his lunch, would she feel a little less in his debt? He opened his mouth, but she interjected, "I insist. Otherwise, I'll get a sandwich from the vending machine."

"Okay, okay. Where do you want to go?"

"I'm treating. You choose."

He beamed and put his arm around her. Obviously her offer of paying for lunch had encouraged him. And she'd meant it to have the opposite effect. Men! They could be so arrogant.

She shrugged out of his embrace and moved up the center aisle a few paces. Glancing back, she saw the disappointment on his face. Let him be disappointed. She refused to lead him on. Lunch and the board's decision and that was it. If she didn't see the pompous, smooth-skinned Galvez again, she wouldn't exactly be devastated.

Relieved was more like it.

***

Manny carried the boxes with his sculptures from his pickup to the booth he was sharing. The other artist, Bill Sanderson, had introduced himself and they'd exchanged greetings. Bill was a self-styled painter who specialized in seascapes. After a few words, they ignored each other while they set up, unlike the women who were sharing booths. If the noise level and laughter was any indication, this was more of a social event than an arts and crafts fair.

Manny was glad they'd paired him with a guy. He couldn't imagine sharing a booth with a gregarious female, especially the first time he was exhibiting his work.

The booths weren't exactly roomy, and he jockeyed for space with Bill. They made several compromises and complimented each other's work. Then they sat in the folding chairs provided and waited for customers. Manny was tempted to ask Bill if this was his first time to exhibit, but he kept quiet, not wanting to give away his inexperience.

LuAnn was their first visitor. Manny had dreaded seeing her again but knew she'd come by. He'd had a hard time getting away from her the other night, and he didn't want a repeat performance.

Sanderson, who looked to be about ten or fifteen years older, was attentive enough for both of them. The age thing again. Among seniors, it was almost like a status symbol—the younger your partner was, the more it elevated your position.

Predictably, LuAnn ignored Bill's overtures and focused on Manny's sculptures, gushing over them. Manny hung back, gritting his teeth, not knowing if her enthusiasm was for his carvings or just another ploy to "bag" him. Thinking about her maneuvering made him feel slightly nauseated. When she was called away abruptly, he breathed a sigh of relief, though she promised to come back later. Maybe he'd pack up and leave early. He wasn't exactly inundated by customers.

In fact, only a couple of people had strolled by while he dealt with LuAnn, and they'd been more interested in Sanderson's paintings—which to Manny's way of thinking looked wimpy. Too many grays and blues with no hint of the brilliant orange sun that warmed the Gulf.

But he was no art critic, and he was probably irritated because no one seemed to appreciate his carvings. He shook his head and tried to ignore his deflated ego. He'd wanted to know how people would react. And he'd told himself he wouldn't care.

Like hell.

Disappointed, he folded his arms and sat down again. Bill hovered at the front of the booth, eagerly trying to draw people in. Manny watched him with a jaundiced eye, determined not to debase himself. After all, he wasn't trying to make a living with his sculptures—they were just a hobby.

Settling back, he closed his eyes, only to be nudged by Bill when a youngish matron with two small children in tow stopped at the booth and examined his carvings. She asked intelligent questions and bought one of his smaller pieces, declaring it would be perfect for her mantle.

When he took her money, his heart expanded and he felt a surge of pride so strong it almost brought tears to his eyes. His first sale. The experience was a heady one. Something he wouldn't forget for a long time.

After that, the rest was easy, the crowd grew and more people stopped by. Not everyone bought something, though there was a lot of interest and he received loads of compliments. Sanderson sold four paintings, and three people bought sculptures.

Around twelve-thirty, he flipped a coin with Bill to decide which one of them would get sandwiches and who would stay with the booth. Manny lost and went to get the sandwiches, leaving Bill in charge. When Manny returned, he was happy to find another of his carvings had sold while he was gone.

Gratified and feeling good about himself, he took stock of the sculptures left—five of the bigger pieces. He made a mental note to concentrate on smaller carvings, as they seemed to be an easier sell. Secretly, he was glad his largest and most expensive piece hadn't sold because it was his favorite.

And if it didn't sell, he'd give it to Catalina. Usually, he wasn't a superstitious kind of guy but for some reason, he felt if the sculpture didn't sell and he gifted it to Cat, it would be a sign. *A sign of what?* He didn't know.

Munching on his sandwich and a bag of chips, he watched as the crowd of shoppers waxed and waned. Around one o'clock the crowd thinned. He made another mental note, realizing he'd sold most of his carvings between eleven and one o'clock when people from downtown could walk over and shop.

He'd surprised himself—he was really getting into the swing of this. There must be arts and crafts fairs back home he could attend.

The crowd parted and Manny swallowed the last bite of his sandwich. Then he saw her—Catalina. And she was heading straight for his booth.

***

Catalina had suffered through lunch at the chic Italian restaurant Galvez had chosen. She'd thought the place pricey and overly pretentious, especially for Brownsville, but she had to admit the food was good.

She had little in common with Galvez, and when they took the time to talk, the disparity was painfully obvious. At least it had been obvious to her. He'd yammered on about his social and political aspirations and the luxury vacations he'd taken during the past two years.

If he'd been trying to impress her, he'd failed miserably. All he'd managed was to irritate her and remind her how different they were.

When they'd finished, she'd glanced at her wristwatch and found they still had plenty of time, as it was barely past one o'clock. She despaired of filling up the next hour, especially with Galvez trailing along.

Then she'd stepped outside the restaurant and caught sight of the striped tents and booths on the grassy lot one block over. Pointing, she'd asked, "What's that?"

He'd shrugged. "Just the old folks' arts and crafts fair. They hold it every year."

"What do you mean by *old* folks? Winter Texans?"

"Mostly—and locals too. It's sponsored by the Valley Senior Recreational Center. Bunch of would-be artists and junk."

"But we've almost an hour and if you don't have anything in mind, I'd like to see it." She gazed at him and smiled, purposely turning on the charm. "I seldom get away from the Park. Anything is a treat to me."

"Oh, okay." He shrugged again and glanced at his watch. "I guess you're right. It beats sitting around the County office."

They'd wandered among the booths, looking at the handicrafts and talking to artists. Galvez had been right—some of the stuff was junk. But a lot of the items were finely crafted and beautiful.

Then she saw him—a big bear of a man—there was no mistaking Manny. He was standing in one of the booths, gulping down a sandwich and surrounded by wooden carvings and paintings.

What on earth was he doing here?

Surprised and curious, she left Galvez and started forward, her feet moving on their own. Like the moon commanded the tides, she moved toward Manny, as if pulled by an invisible current she didn't understand but couldn't resist.

"Hi," Catalina greeted him. "What are you doing here?"

"Selling my sculptures."

"You made these?" A note of disbelief shaded her voice.

Manny shrugged. "I like working with wood."

Her hands caressed a statue of St. Anthony holding a crucifix above his head. "They're so beautiful, Manny, I never knew—"

"Catalina, what are you doing?" Galvez, or the man Manny assumed was Galvez, tapped her on the shoulder. "Why'd you run off like that?"

His tie was askew and his carefully coifed hair stuck out at funny angles. And he was panting, as if he was out of breath.

Half turning toward Galvez, she made the introductions. "Manuel Batista, this is Ricardo Galvez, my attorney. Ricky, this is Manny, he's down from Chicago and rents a space from me.

"And Manny is doing the work around the Park, too." She waved her hand over the sculptures. "As you can see, he's an accomplished craftsman."

Registering Catalina's compliment, his chest swelled and he grew at least another foot.

The attorney nodded and offered his hand. Manny shook his hand, applying pressure and feeling the attorney's bones pop. Galvez grimaced and snatched his hand back. Gratified, Manny smiled inwardly. Galvez narrowed his eyes and shot him a poisonous look.

"This is Bill Sanderson," Manny said. "My booth mate for today. He paints seascapes." He indicated Bill's paintings with a sweep of his hand. Bill stepped forward and offered his hand, first to Catalina and then to Galvez.

"Bill," Manny continued, "meet Catalina Reyes and Ricardo Galvez."

"Pleased to meet you, ma'am, and Mr. Galvez," Bill said.

"Now that's out of the way, it's getting late," Galvez interjected, grabbing Catalina's arm.

Manny clenched his jaw and lowered his head. He didn't like Galvez's tactics. It was all he could do to not tell the attorney to keep his hands to himself.

But Cat shook him off. "Not now, I want to look at this sculpture." Her long, slender fingers rested on Manny's favorite piece, the intricate carving of a seated Madonna holding the Christ child. She lifted the sculpture and gazed at it, turning it over and tracing the details of the faces with her fingertips.

Galvez, standing behind her, snorted and started pacing.

"Manny, this is so beautiful. How much is it?"

He opened his mouth and then closed it. What should he say? Tell her he'd planned on giving her the sculpture. But he didn't want to talk about it in front of Galvez and Bill.

She gazed at him, an expectant look in her hazel eyes. He gripped the counter and searched for an answer. But his gaze strayed downward, drawn to her full, coral-tinted lips.

Damn the sculpture. They could talk about it later. All he wanted was to take her in his arms and kiss her silly in front of Bill and God and everybody—particularly Galvez.

"Catalina?" The attorney tapped her shoulder. "We've really got to go." He pointed at his wristwatch. "The hearing will be back in session."

But she didn't turn to Galvez. Her full attention was on Manny. An invisible thread ran between the two of them, something shimmering and bright. The rest of the world receded, fading away. There was only the two of them, no Galvez, no Bill and no crowds.

Not breaking eye contact with Manny, she said, "But the board has some other cases to hear first. Didn't you tell me that?"

"I did, but—"

"Manny," her voice was barely a whisper, "what do you want for this?" She held up the wooden statue. She gazed into his eyes and then nodded, as if to herself. "You don't want to part with it, do you?"

It was the coward's way out, but he nodded back. He'd explain later, when he gave her the sculpture in a more private setting.

"I understand." Lovingly, carefully, she set the carving back on the counter. "Better put it away so no one else will want it."

"That's a good idea."

"Catalina, we've got to get back to the hearing." This time Galvez tugged on her arm.

Manny dropped his folded arms and dug his hands into the booth's counter. Galvez was damned arrogant, and he didn't like the way he pushed Cat around. A wave of protectiveness washed over him, and he wished Catalina was his—all his.

"I guess we better go, Manny." She nodded in Bill's direction. "Mr. Sanderson, it was nice to meet you."

Bill waved and grinned and turned back to the customer he was waiting on.

Manny leaned over the booth and called out, "Good luck at the hearing."

She stopped and glanced over her shoulder. "*Gracias.* See you at the Park later."

He watched her walk away, her hips swaying under her form-fitting skirt. He clutched the counter harder, digging his fingernails into the wood, risking splinters

Por Dios, he knew they had an agreement, but he couldn't stop wanting her. And his feelings had gone beyond lust. He wanted to spend time with her, wanted to get to know her. In short, he wanted to start a serious relationship with Catalina Reyes.

He just hoped he could convince her he was committed.

***

"Grab that end," Catalina said. "Can't you see I'm struggling here?"

"I've got it. I've got it," Manny said.

Together they stretched the sheet of wallpaper and settled it onto the wall behind the stove. Quickly, before the glue had a chance to dry, they smoothed the surface, eliminating creases and bubbles. Then Manny grabbed the squeegee from his belt and went over the paper, squeezing out excess glue.

Catalina followed behind, wiping the extra glue off the wall with a wet sponge. When she finished, she stood with her hands on her hips, scrutinizing the newly papered wall, looking for mistakes.

"It's fine, Cat," he interrupted her careful study. "Let's get this last piece up."

Spoken like a true man, she thought, impatient when it came to the finishing touches, as if they didn't matter. But they mattered to her. He'd taken such care with the carpentry and the painting. It was almost as if wallpapering was beneath him. She'd offered to do it herself. He'd said it would go much quicker if they did it together, and she'd agreed.

And she was the one who would have to look at these walls for years to come. She didn't want to rush through the job. She wanted the paper to be perfect. Grabbing one end, she followed his lead, and they finished the wall, down to the baseboard, going through the same steps as before.

This time, when she stood back, he joined her and put his arm around her waist. Together, they surveyed the one large room that was her living quarters, taking in the fresh paint and wallpaper, not to mention the new paneling and a marvelous corner pantry complete with a custom-built spice rack on the door. When it came to carpentry, Manny was the best.

Actually, she thought with a surge of affection, he was good at a lot of things. He'd supervised the concrete work outside, catching mistakes and oversights. With his constant surveillance, the subcontractor had finished on time and under budget.

Squeezing his waist in a gush of appreciation, she turned and buried her head in his broad chest, reveling in the pure male smell of him, in the rock-hard muscles beneath her cheek, and the reassuring slow thump of his heart.

He squeezed her, too, half-lifting her off the ground and kissing the top of her head. They'd been like this since the day at the fair. Kind and affectionate with each other, working together without a harsh word between them. They'd kissed and hugged but nothing more. Still, something fundamental had shifted in their relationship. She didn't quite understand what was going on, but they reminded Catalina of an old married couple, loving and comfortable with each other—but no passion.

But she missed the passion.

She didn't know if she was ready for what it entailed, but she missed it anyway. Every night she woke in a tangle of sheets, aroused by erotic dreams of Manny making wild, passionate love to her.

She bit her lip and focused on her home and all the improvements.

"Manny, the kitchen and living room look wonderful! I can't give you enough compliments." She released him and walked to the pantry, throwing the door open. "And the pantry, I love it." She laughed and twirled around, running her fingers over the gorgeous new granite countertops. "And the countertops, too. Everything is so beautiful. I couldn't be happier."

He laughed, too, and shook his head. "I'm glad you're happy, Cat. I aim to please."

She slanted a glance at him. "You sure please me."

Arching one eyebrow, he gave her the look she hadn't seen in the last few days—the lecherous one from beneath half-hooded eyelids. He stroked his jaw. "Now, I could take that in a variety of ways, you know."

"Oh, Manny." She punched him in the shoulder.

"And this is how you show your appreciation? By beating up on me."

"Oh, you…you're so…"

Laughing, he grabbed her and kissed her again. Pulling back, he said, "I think this calls for a celebration."

"Sure. What do you mean?"

"Got anything alcoholic to toast with?"

"I've still got the beers you brought over."

"Then break them out."

"Okay." She crossed to the fridge and pulled out two longnecks, flipping open the caps with a church key.

She handed him a beer. He clinked bottles with her and raised his beer in a toast. "To Catalina's kitchen and living room." He turned up the bottle and downed half of it.

"I'll drink to that." She swallowed her beer, grimacing at the taste. Why did the first swallow of beer always taste so nasty?

"And you're okay to finish the bathroom and bedroom?" he asked, wiping his mouth with the back of his hand.

"What do you mean?"

"Money, Catalina, money. Do you have money for the materials? I know you're saving for your taxes at the end of the year."

She frowned, registering his meaning. She noticed he didn't mention his fee. That had been their only acrimonious exchange—he'd resisted taking her money. But she'd insisted. It was only right.

She still had to be careful about money. The tax board had surprised her and Galvez by taking a middle-of-the-road approach. They'd agreed her property was like the other RV Parks in the area and should be taxed at the same rate, which was lower than the new one originally assessed. But they'd stuck with the higher appraised value because the land was beachfront property, whether she developed it or not. In the end, her taxes had doubled, rather than quadrupled.

It hadn't been the complete victory she'd hoped for, but it was better than nothing. Had she known what the decision would have been, she'd have asked for a bigger loan from the bank. But she hadn't known, and Galvez had been so certain they would win.

Because of the board's decision she was scraping by, trying to finish her home's renovations while saving for the increased taxes. Manny knew about her difficulties, and he was sympathetic. At times, too sympathetic.

"I think I have it under control. The Park is almost full." She smiled at him. "Thanks to you. And the extra revenue should see me through the taxes. I've kept back part of the loan to finish in here."

"Then full speed ahead," he said. "I'll start tomorrow on the bathroom. We've got the whole afternoon to ourselves. What would you like to do?"

She wished they could go for a swim in the ocean; she was gritty and sweaty. But even in the Valley, in February, they'd freeze to death. Then she had a thought.

"I'd like to see you work on your sculptures."

His eyebrows drew together and he frowned. "Let me get this straight. You want to *watch* me carve wood?" He shook his head. "Do you know how boring that is?"

"Not to me."

He gazed at her, and the light in his brown eyes softened. Tipping his beer back, he finished it. "Okay, lady, you're on. But at least let me cook dinner for you. I'm a pretty good cook when I put my mind to it."

"Really?" she teased, emphasizing her disbelief.

"Yeah, and you've never seen the inside of my trailer, either."

That stopped her short, thinking about them alone in his trailer. She knew what would happen. They'd been sidestepping their desire for a long time.

Was she ready?

"I'd love to come to dinner." She answered her own question. "What time do you want me? Can I bring anything?"

***

Manny opened the trailer door at her first knock. She kissed his cheek by way of greeting and handed him the bottle of chardonnay. She was tired of beer, and he'd seemed agreeable to wine.

The Airstream trailer, a classic 1957 Spartanette Tandem, was even smaller inside than she'd imagined. Space was definitely at a premium in these old trailers compared to the modern RVs.

Manny had solved the lack of space by installing scaled-down furniture and lining the walls with cabinets for storage. He also kept the place neat as a pin and utilized bright-colored fabrics as accent items rather than knickknacks.

He noticed her interest. "Want to see the rest of it?"

"Sure."

They were standing in the compact living area. A dining table with a banquette for seating was tucked into the corner between the sofa and kitchen counter. In the back was one bedroom where a large bed took up most of the floor space. Of course Manny would need a large bed—anything smaller and he'd dangle off the end. Completing the trailer's floor plan was a small bathroom with a tiny shower.

"Perfect for one, but I wouldn't want to squeeze two people in here," she remarked.

A funny light came into his eyes. "I just planned for one."

That was blunt enough, she decided. A strange feeling came over her, as if she'd encroached on his private world. She filled up the tense silence by remarking, "You did a lot of work on this Airstream."

"Yeah," he replied. "When I got the trailer, I gutted it and started over."

"I can tell. It's signature Manny." She waved her hand. "All this built-in cabinet space with doors."

"You have to have doors or everything comes spilling out when you're on the road."

"Of course, that makes sense."

A marvelous smell wafted to her from a pot on the stove. "What's cooking?" she asked.

"A special recipe of mine, *pollo para molé verde*."

"Sounds wonderful."

"I hope you like spicy food."

"Love it."

"*Bueno.*" He indicated the sofa. "*Por favor*, have a seat while I pull dinner together. Would you like a glass of wine?"

"That would be great." She sat on the edge of the sofa.

"Coming right up."

He checked the food and uncorked the wine, pouring two glasses. Catalina watched him, admiring the way his big hands cupped the crystal goblets and the way he moved around the kitchen as if he knew what he was doing.

Glancing around, her gaze settled on the table. Manny had outdone himself with the preparations. A snowy white tablecloth covered the functional table tucked into the corner. And on the table were candles, linen napkins, china, silverware, and more crystal glasses. She was impressed with all the trouble he'd gone to. She'd expected to eat off paper plates.

Manny brought her a glass of wine.

"*Gracias.*" Nodding toward the table, she said, "You sure know how to entertain."

He laughed. "Believe me I racked my brain all afternoon, wanting everything to be perfect. My neighbor, Madge, helped me with the china and crystal. I tend more toward Melmac and plastic ware."

Just as she'd thought. But that was practical for a single man, and at least he was honest about it. And he'd gone to the trouble for her, borrowing plates and silverware. His thoughtfulness warmed her.

"Well, I'm impressed." She took a sip of the wine.

"I'm glad."

"When do I get to see you carve?"

"You've got to be kidding."

"No, I meant what I said earlier."

"Okay, how about after dinner. I need to keep an eye on the food."

"That's fine."

"Would you like some music," he offered. "I have a few CDs."

"Wow, you're prepared, aren't you?" She glanced at him from beneath her eyelashes.

He had the decency to flush, his cheeks actually turning pink beneath the dark shadow of his beard. "I don't know what you mean, *Señora* Reyes," he replied with mock formality.

"Oh, I think you do." She lifted one shoulder. "Do you have anything by Celine Dion?"

"Yes, I do."

"That would be great."

She took another sip of wine and paced around the trailer, admiring the built-in cabinets, while he fiddled with the CD player. After a few moments, the strains of *Because You Loved Me*, poured from the speakers mounted near the ceiling.

He stood beside her. When he got this close, she felt weak and her knees went wobbly. She wanted to put her arms around him and hold him tight. They'd formed a truce and they worked well together. But the fierce attraction they felt still simmered beneath the surface.

"How's the music?" he asked.

"Great."

Why had she picked Celine Dion—to torture herself? Celine was known for her torchy love songs. And they didn't really need to add fuel to the fire.

"I think dinner is about ready," he said. "Are you hungry?"

"Starving."

"*Muy bien.*" He went back to the kitchen. "Please have a seat." He opened the fridge and pulled out a salad. Then he opened the simmering pots and pans, spooning food into serving dishes.

Manny was so nice, attractive and handy to have around. Why did he have to be from Chicago? Why did he have to go away? She ducked her head and forced her negative thoughts aside.

Dinner was wonderful, as she'd thought it would be. They started with a green salad garnished with sliced avocados and *piñon* nuts. Then he served her *pozole*, a piquant pork-hominy soup. She couldn't compliment him enough on the soup, and she asked him for the recipe.

The chicken *molé* tasted just as heavenly as it had smelled, served on a bed of saffron rice with stir-fried veggies on the side. If she closed her eyes, she'd think she was in a fancy restaurant.

And the wine flowed, making the dinner perfect. When they'd finished her bottle, Manny produced a second bottle of chardonnay and they kept drinking and talking and eating and laughing.

When she couldn't eat another bite of food or drink another sip of wine, she pushed her plate back. "That was wonderful. But I'm stuffed. And don't expect a dinner invitation from me anytime soon. I'll be hard-pressed to compete."

He smiled and reached for her hand. "I'm glad you liked dinner, but I didn't mean for this to be a competition." He shook his head. "I guess I scuttled my own boat."

She gazed at him, not really hearing his words, registering the husky timbre of his voice. Savoring the feel of his hand holding hers. There were golden flecks in the deep-brown chocolate of his eyes. The candles picked up the gold and made them sparkle. *Madre de Dios*, how she loved his eyes. She didn't think there was another man with softer or kinder eyes.

"Earth to Catalina," he said.

"Oh, sorry." She blushed and dropped her head. Wanting something to do, she fiddled with the stem of her wineglass.

"Do you want some more wine?" he asked.

"No, I couldn't. I would explode."

"I guess you didn't save room for dessert. I have *sopapillas* with honey."

"I can't eat another thing, but don't throw the *sopapillas* out. I'll eat them tomorrow." She snagged his gaze and smiled.

He remembered and returned her smile. "How about for breakfast?"

She knew exactly what he meant. But she hadn't expected the direct approach. And she didn't know how to respond.

"I asked you about your family the last time, but as I recall, you sidetracked me and I told you my life story," she remarked. "When are you going to fill me in?"

Squeezing her hand, he broke eye contact. "There's not much to tell. I've led a pretty average life."

"Oh, come on, Manny, don't be so humble."

"Okay, okay. Let's see, my folks originally came from Matamoros but they moved the family north when I was about ten. My father worked in the steel mills and made a good living. Better than he could have done on the border."

"I didn't realize you were from around here." A tiny seed of hope took root in her heart. *What if Manny wanted to stay?*

"I still have an aunt and cousins across the border. I've been meaning to look them up. Just haven't had the time."

His casual observation stung. He hadn't had the time because she'd kept him busy with the Park. In fact, she'd stolen his vacation. Thinking about it made her ashamed. But he'd practically begged for the job, saying he was bored. Still, she owed him some consideration.

"Please, Manny, don't worry about the rest of my house, go and see your relatives."

"Thanks, I will. But I'd rather finish first."

She shrugged. "Suit yourself. You know I appreciate it."

"I know, and it makes me happy to see you happy."

His declaration touched her heart. They weren't exactly words of love, but they would do for now.

"Did you always want to be a carpenter?" she asked.

"I always knew I wanted to make things with my hands. From the time I was fifteen I worked construction during the summers. I enjoyed working with wood, so that's what I concentrated on when I graduated. I got a job as a carpenter's apprentice."

"Didn't you mention your oldest son has followed in your footsteps?"

"Not exactly, Pablo likes the administrative end of the business. He's not as keen to work with his hands."

"But that's all right, isn't it? It frees you to do what you like best."

"You could see it that way." He shook his head. "Sometimes, though, I think my son needs to get his hands dirty to know how to be a good manager."

She didn't know what to say. Manny didn't appear prepared to let go of the business because he didn't feel his son was ready. If that was true, he'd return to Chicago. Her hopes and heart sank.

"How many children do you have?" she asked

"Four."

"If Pablo is taking care of your business, what do your other children do?"

"My oldest girl, Rita, is married with her first baby on the way. She's a housewife but she's worried about money, so she may get a part-time job after the baby is born."

"It's hard on young couples. But, then, it was hard when Nieto and I were starting a family."

He nodded. "My other two finished college. They have good jobs but haven't settled down." He tugged on his earlobe. "Kind of ironic—the ones who can afford to have a family stay single. And the other two—"

"Your youngest kids sound like mine. They both have good jobs but aren't looking to get married. I envy you having a grandbaby on the way."

"And two other grandchildren." He grinned.

"Pablo's?"

"*Sí*. Juan Luis is eight and Marta is six."

"Lucky you. Do you have pictures?"

"Are you sure you want to see them?"

"But of course."

He got up and fetched his computer from one of the cabinets. He booted up the computer and opened a digital photo album. Handing her the computer, he said, "Knock yourself out. This file has all the pictures of my grandbabies from the time they were born."

She scrolled down the screen and looked through the pictures devoted to his family and grandchildren. There were dozens of screens with numerous pictures. He obviously doted on his family, and she was fooling herself if she thought he would leave them and move here.

She clicked on a series of pictures, asking who was who and the ages of his children and grandchildren in the pictures. He leaned over and answered her questions, giving her a running commentary on his family.

With a sinking heart, she glimpsed the joy suffusing his features when he talked about his kids and grandbabies. And she couldn't blame him. His grandchildren were darlings, and his boys were handsome and the girls attractive.

"You've got a great family, Manny. And still growing. You and your wife must have started young like Nieto and I did."

He straightened and took his seat across from her again, crossing his arms over his chest. There it was again. She'd trampled on forbidden ground. What had she said? For her, given what had happened, talking about Nieto could be painful. Had something happened in Manny's marriage, too? This was the third time he'd avoided the subject.

The way he closed off that part of himself wasn't easy to understand, but she had to respect his feelings. She was getting in way over her head. She couldn't compete with his family and business. And she wanted more than an affair.

No, a fling wouldn't be enough. His leaving would tear her heart out.

And then it hit her. She'd never felt like this since she'd fallen for Nieto. Never known a man who could make her want something more than her children and the Park.

The reality was painful to face—painful and confusing and heart-wrenching.

She was falling in love with Manuel Batista.

Chapter Nine

Catalina rose and put her napkin on the table. "Thank you for a lovely dinner, Manny. But it's getting late. I'm sure you'll want an early start tomorrow."

Manny got to his feet, surprised Catalina was leaving. What had happened? They'd been talking about his family and looking at pictures and...

Then he realized the problem. At the mention of his wife, he'd clammed up. He hadn't meant to react that way, but it was second nature. For a long time, he'd shied away from talking about Lydia, not wanting any painful reminders. Like a thorn in his flesh that had scabbed over, he dared not poke at it because if he did, the anguish would start again.

But he'd made his penance, and his feelings ran deep for Catalina. He wanted her like he'd never wanted another woman, not even his wife. He knew they faced challenges, like long-distance dating. But he didn't care. He would do anything to be with her.

Por Dios, was he falling in love?

He touched her shoulder. "Don't go yet. It's still early. I thought you wanted to see me carve."

His gaze snagged hers, and he could see her hesitate. The push and pull going on inside of her. "But it's dark. Don't you carve outside?"

"Usually." He shrugged. "I don't mind bringing the stuff inside."

"Are you sure?"

"Please, stay." He squeezed her shoulder. "Give me a minute."

"Okay." She crossed to the sofa and sat down. Then she sprang up like a jack-in-the-box. "Why don't I clear the table while you set up?"

"No, I'll do that." He shook his head. "You're the guest."

"It will be quicker if I do it."

He couldn't argue with that. But why was she in such a hurry? He had hoped they would have plenty of time. All night—if his wish came true.

"Okay, suit yourself. I appreciate the help. *Por favor*, just stack the dishes in the sink. The napkins and tablecloth go in the laundry bin."

Nodding, she gathered the silverware and glasses.

He went outside and brought in his latest carving, along with his hand tools. Then he spread old newspapers over the floor. Glancing up, he found she'd cleared the table and was waiting.

"Where do you keep your finished sculptures?" she asked.

"Underneath the trailer in storage. Why?"

"I wanted to see the one from the fair again."

"The Madonna and Christ child?"

"Yes." She wet her lips with her tongue. Seeing the quick darting of her pink tongue, he shut his eyes, keeping a tight rein on himself.

Forget the sculptures and carvings and hand tools and...everything else. All he wanted was to take her in his arms and kiss her until she had to come up for air. Kiss her—kiss her until they were both panting with passion. Until nothing else mattered.

"You only carve religious subjects?" she asked.

"*Sí*, that's what comes to me." He'd never questioned his bursts of inspiration or wondered why he picked religious themes.

But gazing at her, he could imagine sculpting her in wood, nude from the waist up, like the mermaid prow of those old-fashioned sailing ships, her breasts thrust forward, proud and beautiful. A mermaid who lived by the sea.

Rising, he said, "Let me get the sculpture for you."

"You don't need to do that."

He went outside again, brought back the carving, and handed it to her. "The sculpture is yours, Cat. And I don't want your money. It's a gift."

She cradled the carving and an astonished look crossed her face. "I can't accept this. Not after everything you've done. And you said it was your favorite."

"That's why I want you to have it."

Her eyes glistened and one lone tear slid down her cheek. Realizing how deeply he'd touched her, he couldn't remain detached any longer. He needed her, needed to hold her. Gently, he took the sculpture from her hands, put it on the coffee table and folded her into his arms.

They stood like that for a long time, holding each other tightly, swaying a little. He kissed the top of her head and stroked his hands up and down her back, comforting her, reassuring her that he cared.

With her face buried in his chest, her words were muffled, "It's painful for you to talk about your wife. Isn't it?"

"*Sí*."

"I'm sorry."

"Don't be."

She reached up and traced his lips with her fingers.

He kissed the palms of her hands and then he trailed his lips up her bare arms. She gasped and closed her eyes, leaning back in the circle of his arms. He cupped her face and pressed his lips to hers. She tasted of vanilla and spices. Her lips were warm and moist and soft beneath his.

He drank her in, trying to get his fill. His lips moved over hers, coaxing and tempting her at the same time. He pulled her toward the sofa.

Catalina clung to Manny, glorying in the feel of his mouth on hers. Her body thrummed from his kisses, from the firm pressure of his lips and the thrust of his tongue. Their mouths fit together, hand-in-glove, as if they'd been created for each other and had waited all these years to find the other part of themselves.

They tumbled together on the sofa, their mouths hot and wet and clinging, devouring each other. Manny's hands on her arms burned her flesh. And her whole body was flushed with heat and longing.

She combed her hands through his straight brown hair and drew him closer. Her breasts ached and throbbed, begging for his touch. And a thread of fiery desire ran from her erect nipples to between her thighs.

Empty, she was empty, so empty. She wanted him, needed him. Inside of her, filling her.

She didn't know if she was ready to take a lover, knowing he'd be leaving to return to his family.

Oh, but her body was more than ready.

She squirmed on the sofa, feeling the wetness between her thighs slicking her panties. And more than that, more than just the physical, she'd missed being held by a man, being caressed, cherished...

Three long years, over three years, since a man had touched and held her. Until Manny had come into her life.

That last year of her marriage, Nieto hadn't wanted her. She hadn't thought much about it then, trying to juggle all the responsibilities in her life, struggling to keep her head above water. She had made certain to go home as much as possible, but both her children had been away at school. And Nieto had been...Nieto. The man she'd known since she was a teenager. Their marriage was rock solid. Or so she'd thought.

Why hadn't she recognized the signs?

She needed Manny, needed to feel loved again, if only for a few weeks. They were both grownups. Would it be so terrible to find a little comfort, to allow herself the pleasure of passion, after the long, dry desert of the past few years?

Having made her decision, she rained kisses on his brow, his cheeks, and ears. Wanting to take the initiative, she trailed her fingertips lower and found the fly to his pants. She grasped the tongue to his zipper and pulled down.

The CD had ended, and the sound of his zipper reverberated in the quiet room.

Manny raised his head and gazed into her eyes. He covered her hand with his and gently lifted it. Frowning, he zipped his slacks.

"I can't, Cat." He shook his head. "I can't do this. Not unless...until you know..." He covered his face with his hands.

A cold feeling settled in her stomach, almost as if a premonition. Confused, she scooted backward on the couch.

What had happened? She thought he wanted her.

He uncovered his face, and he glanced at her and then looked away. "I haven't told you everything, Cat. That's why I don't like to talk about my late wife." He hesitated. "I cheated on Lydia—all of our marriage, once the children started coming. I didn't go out looking for it, but if a woman, if a woman..."

She gasped, and her mouth dropped open. Her limbs felt numb, and her stomach clenched. She covered her mouth with one hand. She couldn't believe what she was hearing. If he hadn't told her, she would have never believed it.

Were all men cheaters?

His eyes were turned down and he frowned. "I know it sounds terrible, and I'm not trying to make excuses, but my father did the same thing to my mother." He held up one hand, palm out, as if to stop her before she rebuked him. "And I know that's no excuse." He shook his head again. "Lydia was busy with the children, and I thought she didn't know...or didn't care." He rubbed his hand over his face. "But her best friend told me she knew, about a year before she died. And her friend told me how much Lydia suffered when she guessed I had another...another woman."

He raised his head and looked into her eyes. "The other women were just...flings. Never lasted more than a month or so. I was never emotionally engaged." His shoulders slumped, curling inward. "I rationalized my infidelities, of course, telling myself the women meant nothing to me. And that I worked so hard and didn't drink much or gamble or mistreat my family. I told myself I deserved a little fun, a little—"

She covered her ears. "Stop, stop it! *Por favor*, please, I don't want to hear it."

He cradled his hands between his knees and leaned forward. "I know you can hear me, Catalina. And I've told you the worst part. Please, please, listen to the rest."

She turned away from him and buried her face in the sofa cushion.

"I went to my wife on my hands and knees and confessed and asked for her forgiveness. I vowed never to look at another woman." His voice was husky with pain.

She lifted her head and stared at him. But he dropped his eyes again and avoided looking at her.

Could she believe him—did she want to believe him? Did it matter?

"We went to our parish priest and began weekly counseling. It was helping over time. Almost a year went by before Lydia would let me touch her again...in that way. And then just as I thought we were getting our marriage back together, she went out one snowy night for some groceries and...and hit a patch of black ice. She hit a wall and the airbag didn't inflate. She...she died before the ambulance got there."

Catalina shot to her feet. Disgust made her limbs rigid. She wanted to curse, but she refused to give him the satisfaction. She twisted her hands and then rubbed them on her slacks. "Stop! Stop!"

He looked up at her and held out his arms.

Pain ricocheted through her. She wanted to slap him and tell him what an evil, double-dealing *bastardo* he was. But she didn't. Instead, she picked up his carving from the coffee table and looked at it. Drawing her arm back, she threw the sculpture against the trailer wall and mocked him with, "Looking for absolution, Manuel? Looking for pity and forgiveness? Do you think making religious carvings will absolve you?"

He grabbed for her hand, but she pulled away.

"No, no, I don't expect my carvings to... Catalina, I haven't touched another woman in over five years until you. I wanted to do a proper penance for my wife and it only seemed right." His chin trembled and his eyes pleaded. "But when I saw you and got to know you, I couldn't help myself. I wanted you, but I haven't absolved myself, only—"

"*Por favor*, don't even go there." She shook her head. "I don't want to hear any more. Don't say it, don't even think it!" Her voice was shrill, and she trembled as if she had a fever. "I don't want to be your latest conquest."

"But Catalina, it's not like that. You're special, you're—"

"Yeah, that's what Nieto told me, too. I'm special." She brushed past him, ran to the door, and pulled it open. Her heart was heavy, and her chest felt as though steel bands constricted it. "You'll find no forgiveness from me, Manuel Batista. My Nieto cheated on me—that last year of our marriage." She stared at him and clenched her hands. "And he had plenty of rationalizations, too. I wasn't home enough. I didn't care about him and the kids." Her voice pitched higher, bordered on screaming. She lowered her voice. "Yeah, he had lots of reasons, like I only cared for the Park. That he was lonely and needed a woman..." She stopped herself and turned her head to one side.

Manny got to his feet and approached her. "Don't go, Catalina. I didn't know about you and your husband." He shook his head and held out his arms. "I'm sorry, so sorry, I didn't know about your marriage. But I wanted to tell you the truth about my marriage and my past before we...before we..."

She slammed the door in his face. And ran sobbing to her home.

***

Manny tucked the Madonna and Child sculpture under one arm and Catalina's purse under the other. He eased open the front door of the RV office and grabbed the bell to keep it from ringing. He was surprised the door wasn't locked this early in the morning.

Moving quietly, he crossed the office and went behind the counter. Any moment he expected Catalina to come in and ask him what he was doing. He glanced over his shoulder, but the A-frame building was quiet, no one was moving around, not even *Migo*. Some watchdog.

Putting her purse and the sculpture beneath the counter, he was certain she'd find them. She'd thrown his sculpture away last night, but he hoped she would change her mind. If not, and she threw it away again, he couldn't blame her. And in the heat of last night's revelations, she'd forgotten her purse, too.

His gaze fell on a pad and pencil. He thought about leaving her a note, but he hesitated. What would he say? Especially after last night. He could explain he was going to visit relatives in Matamoros. Tell her he wouldn't be around for a while. But after the way he'd unintentionally hurt her, he didn't know if she would care.

Not now. Maybe in time. But did they have time?

He needed to give her time to sort things out. Just as he'd spent a sleepless night—trying to sort out his feelings. He couldn't blame her for her reaction, especially after what had happened to her. But he wished she would have listened carefully to him and not just reacted.

He had changed; he knew he had. If he and Catalina were in a relationship, he would never cheat on her—no matter how much distance separated them. He just wished she would give him a chance. Put aside the past, as he'd tried to do, by telling her everything, and get on with their lives. *Was it too much to ask?*

He slipped out the door again and climbed into his pickup. Putting the car into gear, he drove away, heading south to México. When the Park faded into the background, he sighed.

Gripping the steering wheel, his thoughts continued to tumble. He couldn't shut them off. He was hoping new experiences, like visiting his relatives in México, would give him something else to think about.

Por Dios, had he been wrong to tell her the truth?

She'd been hot and ready for him. She'd even unzipped his slacks. She'd never done that before, had always waited for him to take the initiative. So, why had he picked that particular time to tell her the truth? Because he wanted their relationship to start with a clean slate? Knowing what he knew now about her marriage, would he have confessed his failings?

Yes, to keep his vow to himself. No more casual sexual encounters. He cared about Cat and wanted a lasting relationship. How that would work out, he wasn't certain. But he knew he'd done the right thing, telling her.

He'd known she didn't want a casual affair. He shook his head. Telling her about his previous casual affairs had only fueled her doubts and fears. But if he was the new man he believed he was, he couldn't have done it any other way.

Por Dios, his thoughts were going in circles, getting him nowhere.

He straightened his shoulders and gripped the steering wheel. He'd done the right thing, the only thing. Now it was Catalina's turn. Could she overcome her past and move forward?

But was he being completely honest with himself, even now? Was he ready to remarry? Hell, he'd never even considered remarrying. The thought hadn't occurred to him, but that was probably what she wanted.

Or to be fair, maybe she would settle for a long-term relationship. But that would be difficult, too. In a few short weeks, he'd be returning to Chicago. Returning to his family and seeing Rita's first child born. Holding that tiny scrap of humanity in his hands, in awe of the miracle of life.

But what about the miracle of love?

Did Catalina love him? Did he love her? Was it possible to find someone to love after all this time, after thinking no one could replace Lydia? He didn't know. He thought he might love her, but what could they do about it, even if she forgave him? How to bridge hundreds of miles between her home and his?

He was attracted to Catalina and enjoyed her company. They worked well together and when they kissed...the chemistry between them was hot. Hotter than it had been with Lydia.

Was that love?

And if he did want to marry Cat, where would they live? His family was in Chicago, and they were close. Catalina didn't seem particularly close with her kids. But she'd never leave the Park. The Park was her dream, and she'd sacrificed everything for it. Even her husband.

Seeing the sign pointing to México, he exited the highway and followed the markers. When he saw the sign proclaiming, "*Bienvenidos a México,*" he relaxed and tried to put Catalina from his mind. It had been a long time since he'd returned to the country of his birth, and he was looking forward to visiting his relatives.

But he couldn't quit thinking about her. He cared for her. How much, he wasn't certain. And given what she'd been through with her husband, he could understand if she was afraid of getting involved and hurt again.

After all, he'd been avoiding emotional pain for years. But that wasn't how he wanted to live anymore. He wanted Catalina in his life. How he would go about it—he had no idea.

***

Catalina closed her robe and belted it. She ran to the window and saw the tail lights of Manny's pickup disappear. The sun had barely peeked above the horizon, and he was already gone.

Not that she could blame him. After last night, she didn't know how she could face him. The situation was impossible. He was a self-proclaimed cheater, and that was what had broken up her marriage with Nieto.

She crossed her arms at her waist and hugged herself. Not that Nieto was a cheater like Manuel. He'd been driven to it. She should have put Yolanda in a nursing home and paid more attention to her husband and family. What had happened was her fault.

How many times had she been over this in her head? She'd done what she thought was right at the time. And Nieto had done what he needed to do.

This was life, not a morality play. People did what they felt they needed to do.

So when would she quit blaming herself for wrecking her marriage?

She shook her head and bit her lip, tasting the coppery flavor of her own blood.

She needed to sort out what was important and what wasn't. And she needed to let go of her guilt. She'd hung onto it for a long time. Maybe she'd made some wrong decisions, taking care of Yolanda and keeping the Park. But her decisions had seemed right at the time.

And Nieto had made his own decision. Instead of coming to her and telling her he wanted her at home, he'd taken the easy way out and found another woman.

If she'd been wrong, hadn't Nieto's decision been worse? Selfish and unfeeling? Jettisoning their marriage and vows after so many years?

But what of Manny? At least he'd told her the truth about his marriage. He didn't have to do that. She would have never known. And she'd been ready to go to bed with him.

He'd shown more courage than her husband of twenty-something years.

Even if she could forgive Manny and take him as a lover, he was still a man. Sex meant something different to a man. Would he stand by his vow, as he'd told her, and make their relationship special and committed?

She crossed to the counter and looked around, wondering if he might have left a note. She saw her purse and the sculpture beneath the counter.

So he had been here. Something, a sixth sense, had told her he'd come and gone. Silently, she thanked him for returning her purse. She'd worried about it last night, but she couldn't go back and face him.

And the sculpture.

She was surprised he'd left it, especially considering she'd thrown it against his trailer wall and mocked him about his choice of religious subjects. Thinking about it, her eyes burned and she wiped a tear away. As long as she had the carving, she'd never forget him.

Never forget what might have been.

She went back into her home, taking the purse to her bedroom and giving the Madonna and Christ child a place of honor on her new mantle. She fed *Migo*. Then she made coffee and drank it at her new table. After she'd dressed, she wandered around the downstairs room. She was so accustomed to having Manny around, the one room echoed with loneliness.

Migo, who was following her aimless wandering, lifted his head when he heard the tinkling bell. Excited, they both started up, hoping it would be Manny. But it was Mr. McCall, come to see if he had any mail. But he didn't. He was one of the few renters who never received mail

Mr. McCall was Manny's friend and neighbor. Maybe he would know where Manny had gone. She was tempted to ask him but couldn't bring herself to do it. What would he think? Would he gossip with her other renters? She didn't want her relationship with Manny exposed.

She smiled and made small talk instead. After that, the morning got busy with people coming and going. New renters came and took the last available slots, and then there was a crisis in the laundry room.

Returning from the laundry room, *Migo* trailed behind her, his tail between his legs and his ears flattened. Glancing at him, she knew how he felt. He'd grown accustomed to having Manny around. She looked for the hundredth time at his space.

His Airstream stood perched over the slab, but his truck wasn't there.

The afternoon dragged by. Catalina was tempted to close up the place and visit Elena. She needed a shoulder to cry on. *Migo* moped around, whining, making her feel Manny's loss that much more.

With a full camp, she hesitated, not comfortable with closing the Park and leaving. Instead, she contented herself with calling Elena and pouring her heart out. Her best friend wasn't much help, though Catalina appreciated her sympathetic ear.

Night fell and with the darkness, loneliness and dread swamped her. His pickup was still missing. Where could he have gone? Was he staying away all night?

She ran a bath and soaked. She tried to read and watch television, but the only thing that interested her was Manny's missing truck. At midnight, she couldn't stand it any longer. She wished she would have thought to get his cell number, but there had been no need. He'd always been around.

Rummaging through her office, she found a clean piece of stationery, a pen, and an envelope. She sat for a long time, composing her note. What could she say? Was she willing to risk being hurt?

Anything was better than the way she felt now.

Finally, she kept the note short and sweet, apologizing for not hearing him out and for not being more understanding about how he'd changed. She added a postscript, inviting him to dinner when he returned. Surely he would know what she meant by that. She flushed, wondering if she should spell it out for him.

Shaking her head, she couldn't do that. He'd have to divine her message—she was willing to take him on his terms.

Was that what she wanted?

No, but if it was the only way she could have him, even for a few short weeks, it was better than nothing. Better than this gnawing loneliness, wondering where he was and who he was with.

She stuffed the note in the envelope and scrawled his name on the outside. She grabbed a roll of scotch tape and a flashlight and went to his space, taping the note on the door of his trailer.

Even though she knew he wasn't home, she paused, listening and hoping. Maybe he had taken his pickup to the shop and hitched a ride back and she'd missed him. But his trailer was quiet and dark.

***

Two long and endless days later, Catalina was putting the mail in the slots when she happened to glance outside and see Manny's pickup roar by.

Her chest felt tight, her stomach knotted, and her ears burned.

Every curse word she knew crowded her head, but she didn't say them. Instead, she clenched her fist and pounded the counter. *Migo* raised his head and barked. She ignored her dog. She'd suffered during the past few days and didn't know how she felt about Manny any more.

Perdición take the man, why had he bothered to come back? Three days of endless worry and nagging doubts had taken their toll. Her loneliness had turned to utter despair and fear for his safety. And then slowly, imperceptibly, her feelings had changed.

He hadn't called and he hadn't left a note. Who did he think he was—to treat her that way? She didn't know where he'd gone or what had happened to him. For all she knew, he could be lying dead in a gutter somewhere. The faces of his family had haunted her. And she'd wondered how she could tell them, how she would break the news their father and grandfather was...

She was done with Manuel Batista. If he cared so little for her, then she wanted him gone. He could hitch up his trailer and leave today and she'd gladly refund his money. Stiffening her spine, she crossed her arms over her chest and waited. He had a pile of mail from home. He would come to the office.

Then she remembered—the note she'd left.

¡Maldita sea! She couldn't let him read her note. Her feelings had circled one hundred and eighty degrees since she'd written it. She didn't want him on any

terms. Didn't want him to finish the work or come to dinner. All she wanted was for him to be gone from her Park and her life.

Rushing out the front door, she sprinted to his space. When she arrived, he'd just pulled the envelope from his door and stood holding it. She wasn't too late. Almost, but not quite.

She stuck her hand out, palm up. "That's mine. If you would please return it."

He swung around and gazed at her. He frowned and the look in his eyes was wary. But she didn't care what he was thinking or how he felt. She wanted the damned note.

"Buenos días a ti." He inclined his head and glanced at the envelope. "You say it's yours, but it has my name on it."

She gritted her teeth. "I wrote it to you. And now I've changed my mind, and I want it back." She stretched out her arm again with her hand open.

He stood on the top step and she was at the bottom. He towered over her. With the addition of the steps, she had to crane her neck to see his face.

He pushed past her and strolled toward his pickup, tearing the envelope open. "It must be something important for you to put up such a fuss. I better take a look."

"That's my private property," she hissed, running after him.

"Then why'd you tape it to my door?"

She shook her head and grabbed for the envelope. He jerked his arm back. She missed and loosed a string of curse words.

He raised his index finger. "Temper, temper. I thought you were going to work on that, Catalina."

"You have no right to lecture me."

Red dots danced before her eyes. She lunged for the note again, and he quickly transferred it to his other hand. He smiled a self-satisfied smile.

¡Coño! How she hated him!

He took the note from the envelope and shook it out. She lowered her head and charged, butting him in the stomach. His eyes went wide and he grunted. She grabbed for the note again. But he recovered quickly and stepped back.

Adrenaline pumped through her body, and rage filled her heart. She refused to give up.

They began a slow dance.

She pursued him, leaping and spinning, trying to snag the note from his hand. He feinted and stepped sideways, the cursed piece of paper fluttering out of reach. When she got hold of the note, she'd tear it up and scratch his damned eyes out.

But he was too quick for her, too powerful and too tall. When she rushed him, he merely retreated a few steps or turned his body to the side, keeping the paper behind him. What she was trying to do was useless and stupid. And she hoped none of her renters were watching.

Thinking about her renters, she realized how ridiculous she must look. Her breath came in pants and perspiration covered her. She thought she might be sick. Leaning over, she clasped her knees with her hands, dragging air into her lungs. After a few moments, she straightened.

Manny stood a few steps away, reading the note.

She groaned and wiped her forehead with the back of her hand.

He held up the paper. "Here's your note, Catalina." He gazed at her. "Did you mean what you wrote?"

With his gaze on her, she cringed, realizing how she must look with no makeup, her unwashed hair skinned back in a ponytail, and her face ravaged by tears and sleepless nights.

"When I wrote it." She shook her head. "Not now."

"What made you change your mind?"

"Are you crazy, asking me that?" She planted her fists on her hips and stared at him. "You left for three days without a word. What if something had happened to you? What if I had to notify your family—?"

"Catalina, *por favor*, let's leave my family out of this. This is between you and me. You know why I left. You were angry and didn't want to listen—"

"You could have called so I wouldn't have worried."

He rubbed his hand over his jaw. "You're right, but I didn't know if you wanted to hear from me. I'd hoped the time apart would give you the opportunity to reflect on what I was trying to tell you the other night."

She took several deep breaths and tried to calm her racing heart. There was some truth to what he said. She could see why he'd stayed away and hadn't called. Unfortunately, he didn't understand her. She was quick to anger and quicker to forgive. And she was a worrier. Her children could vouch for her tendency to worry. When his absence had stretched into three days, she'd driven herself crazy with horrible visions about what might have happened.

She shook her head. Why had she thought she could have a relationship with a man who didn't understand her basic nature? There was nothing left to say.

Her eyes burned, but she refused to start crying again. Especially in front of Manny. Holding both palms out, she shook her head again. Then she turned on her heel and walked away. But she heard his footsteps on the gravel behind her. He grasped her shoulder and gently pulled her around.

"Do you want me to finish your house?" he asked.

"I would prefer not." She shook his hand off. "Actually, I want to refund your rent and have you clear out."

"Just because I didn't call you?"

"That's the tip of the iceberg, Manny. You didn't understand your wife and how she felt and you don't understand me…" She stopped herself. What was the use? And she shouldn't have brought up his wife, either. It wasn't her place.

"So I don't understand you. Okay, I'll bite. What don't I understand?"

"Oh, forget it."

"But I don't *want* to forget it." He tugged on his earlobe. "Maybe I shouldn't have teased you about the note and given it back. I'm sorry, but you were so angry and I thought you'd wear yourself down." He shook his head. "And I was disappointed too. When I saw how angry you were, I wished I'd come back sooner or…called. I guess I blew it."

"*Sí*, you blew it."

"Would it help if I told you I went to Matamoros to visit my relatives? Remember I mentioned I had relatives on the other side of the border."

"I remember. But three days without a word? I worried and…" She grimaced. "You don't want to hear this."

"Yes, I do. And I didn't want you to worry. But when I left—"

"You were upset because I didn't want to listen and because I didn't believe you'd changed, so you didn't feel like calling me. Am I right, Manny? You said you thought I wouldn't take your call, but if you'd really wanted to reach out to me—"

"You're right, Cat. You needed time to think. I needed time to think." He looked down. "I didn't know you'd worry. It didn't occur to me." He rubbed his chin again. "Though, I should have known. Lydia was a worrier, too. And Rita… Let's just say my oldest daughter could probably out worry you. I just didn't think. And I felt like a call from me would only muddy the water." He raised his hand as if he would caress her cheek and then dropped it. "I wanted you so badly, but I wanted to be truthful with you, too. I guess when you reacted the way you did, it hurt me. You had every right to feel that way. But I didn't know what to think, so I decided we needed some time apart." He shook his head. "I want to understand where you're coming from, Cat. That's why I opened myself and my past to you. I wanted us to start out right."

His gaze fastened on her.

She flinched under his steady gaze and turned away. "I opened myself, too, Manny, telling you about Nieto. And now I've had time to think, I don't know where we go from here." She lifted her head and met his gaze. "I don't know if I'm ready to trust a man again, especially after—"

"I told you what happened to my marriage." He sighed. "It was a risk I had to take, Cat. Otherwise, my vow and the six years I've spent trying to change would have meant nothing. I did a lot of thinking too." He wiped his perspiring brow with the back of his arm.

"I know you don't want to hear it... not now. But I care for you...and not just in a physical way." He reached out for her again and touched her arm. "I missed you, Cat, even though I was surrounded by my relatives. I tried to stop thinking about you but couldn't. And I'm sorry I made you worry." He laughed, a brittle laugh. "Come to think of it, if you'd known where I'd gone, you might have worried more. México has changed. My relatives feel like they live in a war zone, what with the cartels and all. And I can't say I blame them."

She wrapped her arms around her waist. "Yes, México has changed, and it's too bad. I wish their government would..." She shook her head.

She was talking to fill the silence. She didn't want to acknowledge what he'd said about caring for her. His timing was awful. She didn't know if she could believe anything he said. "Now I'm babbling." She drew an arc in the gravel with the toe of her tennie. "Don't you think it would be simpler if we didn't start, Manny, if you left and went back to Chicago?"

"Maybe." He shrugged. "Sure, it would be easier if we didn't start... But that's not what I want. Though, I understand your feelings...or I'm trying to." He took her hand in his. "Before you banish me, let me finish your home. I don't like to leave a job unfinished." He hesitated. "Unless you've got someone else."

"No, I don't have anyone else."

"Then you'll let me do it? Don't send me away now, Catalina."

She lifted her head and gazed into his soft brown eyes. What was there about this man that she couldn't stay angry with him, that he twisted her around his finger, and made her doubt her better judgment?

"Okay, you can finish. I'll stay in the office and out of your way while you work. But after that—I want you to leave."

He nodded and dropped her hand.

She turned and walked back to the office. She'd done the right thing to safeguard her feelings, asking him to go away. Now if she could find a reason to go on living without him, she'd be fine.

Chapter Ten

Manny worked like a demon, pulling out the old fixtures in Catalina's bathroom and replacing them. He put new tile around the bathtub and on the floor and replaced the ancient medicine cabinet.

True to her word, Catalina stayed out of his way. She spent her time in the office with the door closed or outside in the Park. Even though they weren't on the best of terms, when the remodeling needed to be discussed, they talked about the work but kept their conversations confined to the business at hand.

Migo was Manny's constant companion, lying outside the bathroom and trailing after him when he took breaks. He was becoming so attached to the Lab he was considering getting a dog. Rita had called, and she was happy he'd be leaving soon. He couldn't wait to see his family again.

All that stood between him and his family was Catalina's bedroom. Having remodeled the bathroom in such a strained atmosphere, he wondered what had possessed him to want to finish the job. She could have gotten Torres to do it, and he would have been on his way.

Misplaced gallantry or foolish hope, he didn't know. Had he thought Catalina would change her mind?

Hank had dropped by his trailer one night with Esmeralda, asking if Manny wanted to accompany them to a dance. Esme and Hank were dating and so obviously taken with each other, it had been painful to watch them. He hated to admit it, but he'd been envious of Hank, seeing how happy he was.

He shook his head. He wasn't looking forward to renovating Catalina's bedroom. He'd already been up there, and he didn't like what he saw. The loft bedroom had a rickety railing protecting the abrupt drop into the room below. The railing didn't provide any privacy or safety. He wanted to replace it with a wall but wasn't certain if she would like that option. Possibly a half-wall? He needed to talk it over with her.

And talking to Catalina wasn't one of the more pleasant aspects of his job. She'd answer him, but she was so distant and frosty he dreaded interacting with her.

Her bedroom presented him with another problem. It was the most intimate room in her home, complete with the bed she slept in, saturated in her vanilla scent, and with a picture of her late husband sitting on the bureau. Working in her bedroom was going to be sheer torture.

Climbing the stairs to the loft, he glanced around. When he put his hand on the railing, he felt the rotten wood give and jumped back. Something had to be done. He retraced his steps, went to the office door and knocked.

"Come in," Catalina said.

He opened the door and stuck his head in. "Catalina, can I show you something?"

She got up from the desk where she'd been working. "Of course."

They trudged up the stairs together. Manny pointed at the railing. "I want to replace it with a wall. A wall would give you privacy as well as safety. What do you think?"

She lifted her head and looked around. "I think it would close the room up too much. Besides, I don't need privacy." She stared past him. "I live alone.

"As for safety," she walked to the railing and leaned on the top board, "you're right, the wood needs to be replaced."

He took a step toward her, his heart in his throat. Did she know how rotten the railing was? "Catalina, *por favor*, stand away! Don't lean on—"

The sound of cracking wood reverberated like a shot. As if in a dream, he saw the railing splinter. Catalina scrambled and flung out her arms, trying to grab something solid. With a grating screech, the wooden top rail broke off and plunged down.

Catalina, her eyes wide and her mouth open in a silent scream, hung onto the edge for one heartbeat, flailing her arms. Manny lunged and caught her just as she was about to fall over the side.

Sobbing and shaking like a leaf, she clung to him. He held her close and stroked her back, whispering nonsensical, comforting words into her long, curly hair. Carefully, he backed up a step, taking Cat with him, pulling her away from the gaping abyss. He would have released her, but she held onto him with a grip of iron, still trembling.

He couldn't complain. He'd forgotten how sweet her body felt pressed against his. How her curves molded themselves to his frame.

He ran his hands through the russet glory of her hair and smoothed it away from her face. Then he moved his hands to her shoulders and gently massaged her taut muscles. She sighed and went limp, allowing him to cradle her in his arms. With her breasts pressed against his chest and her thighs cupped between his legs, his loins caught fire and he grew hard.

Por Dios, she drove him crazy! He sifted the strands of her silky hair through his fingers. Slowly, tenderly, he let his fingertips trail down her satiny throat. He skimmed the outline of her breasts and then spanned her waist with both hands.

"It's all right. I've got you. You won't fall."

He could feel her body relax, but the pulse at her throat was beating against her translucent skin, fluttering and fast, like the wings of a hummingbird. She wouldn't admit it, but his closeness affected her. He could sense the response in her body—feel the way she melted into his embrace. They stood, folded in each other's arms for a long time, their bodies clinging, allowing the shared warmth to seep into their muscles and bones.

Slowly, tentatively, she lifted her head and looked into his eyes.

"You're okay," he said. "But it was a close thing."

She nodded and kept staring at him, her hazel eyes glistening. She parted her lips and wet them with her pink tongue.

He understood the gesture. And he wasn't going to let the opportunity pass. Dipping his head, he captured her mouth in a long and hungry kiss. So very, very hungry. She tasted of honey and vanilla, and her lips were soft and giving. Her arms encircled him, pulling him closer.

Groaning, he clasped her heart-shaped rear end and filled his palms. He lifted her up and caressed her buttocks. He'd waited forever to touch her there. She had the most perfect ass he'd ever seen on a woman. And he wanted to see her ass naked.

Hell, he wanted to see all of her naked, lying splayed on the bed, waiting for him. Hot and hungry for him.

Devouring her mouth and joining their tongues together, he lifted her higher until she wrapped her legs around his waist. Then she leaned back, secure in the strength of his arms, and rode him, rubbing her crotch against the bulge in his jeans.

He'd never made love to a woman through her clothes. He guessed there was a first time for everything. Her provocative movements, despite the layer of clothing separating them, enflamed him. His penis was extended and rock hard. If he didn't stop her, he'd spill his seed in his jeans.

With her legs still locked around his waist, he crossed to the bed and eased her down on the bedspread. Her eyes were half-closed, heavy-lidded, and her face was flushed. The hard buds of her nipples strained against the stretchy material of her pullover.

She kicked off her sandals and lay on the bed, waiting.

If ever a woman was ready—she was. But he remembered how ready she'd been the last time. This time he'd go slow, firing her desire to such a feverish pitch she wouldn't be able to stop. And he wouldn't stop, either.

This time, there would be no turning back.

He joined her on the bed and propped himself on one elbow. With his other hand, he traced a line from her temple to her chin and back again. She shuddered and kissed the palm of his hand. His hand strayed lower, fluttering over her breasts, brushing the hard nubs of her nipples. Her eyes drifted shut, and she arched her back, begging for more.

He lowered his head and nibbled at the corners of her mouth. His tongue flicked over her lips, wetting them and stroking them. With his hand he traced imaginary circles on her stomach, slowly spreading the circles wider and wider, looping lazy figure eights over her abdomen and lower until he grazed the area between her thighs.

She lurched up and drew his tongue in, sucking it into her mouth. She pressed his hand to her, but he pulled away, knowing what she wanted. Instead he stroked her breasts through the thin material of her pullover, cupping and fondling them.

Moaning softly, she slipped her arms around his neck, drawing him down until he lay sprawled on top of her. He worried his weight was too much for her petite frame, but she didn't seem to mind. Her mouth moved over his in wild abandon while her hands caressed his shoulders and combed through his hair.

Responding to the feverish pitch of her kisses and caresses, he eased his hand beneath her pullover and freed one breast from its lacy prison. Softly, gently, he stroked and fondled the warm fullness of her breast, glorying in her responsive nipple when it puckered into a tight point.

She followed his lead, pulling the shirt from his jeans and tracing her fingertips over his back and chest. Her gentle stroking raised the stakes to another level. He wanted her so badly it hurt. But he wouldn't fulfill their desires until she begged him to.

When she took his hand in hers again and forced it down, he obliged her for a few moments, rubbing the denim material between her thighs. She lifted her hips, urging him on, but he stroked her legs instead, gently drawing his fingertips over the insides of her thighs until he almost touched her before he stroked down again.

She was so excited; he could feel her wetness through the denim of her jeans. He smelled the musky scent of her arousal, and it heated his blood to the boiling point. Moaning into her mouth, he didn't know how much more he could take before he was the one pushed over the edge.

His penis ached and strained against his jeans. He needed to be inside of her.

Without warning, she broke their kiss and lifted one arm while she tugged at the hem of her pullover. Because she'd initiated the action, he helped her pull her top off. Then she sat up and reached behind her back, unhooking her bra.

Her beautiful, rosy breasts swung free, the nipples hard little buds. He stared at her breasts for a long time, drinking in how lovely she was.

"Are you sure you want this, Cat?" As soon as the words left his mouth, he could have kicked himself.

There would be no turning back. He was intent on making love to her. He wanted her, and she wanted him. How long had they waited for this moment, afraid to be intimate, frightened of their pasts and despairing of their futures?

"Touch me, Manny." Her voice was breathless, husky with passion. "I want you to touch my breasts and stroke me all over, and so much more..." Her eyelids drifted shut.

He took a deep breath. "You're so beautiful, *que linda, mi amorcita.*"

He stretched out his hands and caressed her breasts, plucking her sensitive nipples. She bent back, propping herself up with her arms. Lowering his head, he took one breast into his mouth and suckled her and then licked her areola with his tongue.

She lurched up and buried her nails in his shoulders, clinging to him. He suckled and stroked her breasts. They were hot and heavy to his touch.

Her fingers were busy with the buttons of his shirt. When the front of his shirt opened, he shrugged the piece of clothing off.

Catalina pulled him closer, crushing her breasts against his naked chest and rubbing her body against his like a cat. He groaned and tangled his hands in her hair, giving himself over to the sensation of her bare flesh against his.

Their mouths met again, and he thrust his tongue inside. She moaned into his mouth and seized one of his hands, pressing it against her woman's mound again. This time, he cupped her pubis and rubbed the denim against her clit.

After a few seconds, he took his hand away and stroked her naked stomach just to the top of her jeans, teasing her, wanting to bring her to the brink.

Throwing her head back, she gazed at him again, her gray-green eyes dark and stormy with passion, her pupils dilated.

She unbuttoned and unzipped her jeans. The material fell apart, revealing a black, lacy wisp that matched her bra. She raised her hips. Seeing her like this mesmerized him. Watching her, he got so hot and hard, he thought he'd burst and make a fool of himself.

"Help me pull them down," she said.

As if awakening from a deep sleep, he understood what she wanted. What they both wanted. With trembling hands, he slid her jeans down and tossed them on the floor. Only a black triangle of cloth hid her naked body. Though she was petite, her hips were lush and wide, perfect for cradling him when they made love.

Tentatively, he reached out and stroked the soft, lacy material over her crotch. She groaned again and leaned back on her elbows, lifting her hips in a silent invitation.

Not yet, he counseled, not quite yet, he tried to tell himself, even though his penis protested and throbbed. He wanted to imbed himself in her sweetness, drive his penis so deep she'd be imprinted with him forever.

When he took her mouth again and teased her breasts with his fingertips, she tugged at the button on his jeans, unfastening and unzipping them. Her hand found the slit in his boxers and she drew him out. Her warm, soft hand cupping his erection was almost more than he could take.

Rising quickly, he removed his jeans and boxer shorts. She wriggled out of her panties and lay naked on the bed, her legs spread and her knees raised. Hot and wet and ready for him.

Just like his fantasy.

His gaze slid over her creamy skin and luscious curves. She was gorgeous, a dream come true. Seeing the curly auburn hair of her pubis so excited him that he had to grit his teeth to keep from ejaculating. He couldn't believe how much he wanted her and how much she obviously wanted him.

Gazing at Manny, naked and towering over her, the breath lodged in her throat. She'd studied Greek mythology in school and if ever there was a man who looked like her vision of Hercules, Manny was that mythical character.

Gone was the affable bear, *Balu*, to be replaced by the warrior Hercules. He was all hard planes and bulging muscles. His massive chest tapered down to slim hips. His thighs looked like tree trunks, solid and hard. And his penis...

She'd never seen such a large penis in her life. Of course, her experience was limited. But still... Gazing at the dark purple head with one dewy drop of moisture glistening on it, she felt a strange thrill lance through her. Because he was so big, might he hurt her...or would the pleasure be unbelievable?

Leaning down, he retrieved his wallet and took out a plastic-wrapped condom. Watching him, she silently blessed his thoughtfulness. But then, that was Manny, thoughtful and prepared. How had she resisted him for so long?

He tossed the package on the nightstand and lowered himself beside her, running his hands over her body. "When we're both ready, I'll put it on. Okay?"

Nodding, she shuddered under his gentle touch, giving herself over to the wanton pleasure of his hands seeking her most secret places, finding ways to drive her wild with need.

She'd never been so aroused in her life. He'd played with her and teased her and driven her to the brink of insanity. When his fingers strayed downward and explored her wet folds, she arched into his touch, her heels digging into the bed and her hands clutching the chenille spread.

Without warning, the climax burst over her, wave upon wave of ecstasy, spreading through her body, engulfing her, sending her spiraling into a million, trillion stars of pleasure.

She pulled her mouth free and gasped. "Now, *por favor*," she begged. "I want...I want...you inside of me." She reached out and circled his penis with her hand.

"*Amorcita*, I want you, too, more than you know." He lifted his head and stretched one hand toward the nightstand.

She heard the crinkle of plastic and clenched her legs together, not knowing if she could wait. She'd found a kind of fulfillment, but her woman's passage throbbed and pulsed, needing him to fill that empty, aching part of her.

When he rose above her and nudged her thighs apart, she almost fainted with desire. His huge, muscled body strained, glistening with perspiration. He reared back, penis in hand, ready to enter her.

She raised herself up, and he cupped her buttocks in his big, callused hands. Then he entered her with one hard push. The pleasure was swift and incredible. Her vaginal muscles clenched, drawing him in deeper. He groaned and strained, his eyes closed.

He began the rhythm, as old as the sea tides. She took up the rhythm, rocking with him, giving and taking. He was huge, filling her up, burning a path into her belly. A new kind of tension built and built, overflowing her, consuming her.

Together, they climbed the highest mountain, crested the biggest wave, ascended to the farthest star. And when they climaxed together, it was as if they surrendered the essence of themselves and became one—one entity—bright and shining and whole.

Manny collapsed on the bed and pulled her to him. They lay side-by-side, stretched on the bed, every inch of their bodies touching. He picked up a strand of her hair and stroked her bare shoulder with it. "Do you know how happy you've made me?"

Smiling, she snuggled against his chest. "No happier than me."

"Catalina, I—I want you to know how much this means to me." He smoothed her hair from her face. "This isn't just about lust—"

"Isn't it?" she interrupted, holding her breath. Was he going to say he loved her? She hoped so because she wanted to tell him, too, wanted to scream her love from the rooftops.

But only if her love was reciprocated.

If not, he'd think she was trying to tie him down, trying to make him choose between her and his family. And she didn't want him to feel trapped.

He kissed her mouth. "Not just desire, Cat. Do you know how much you mean to me?"

"Tell me," she urged, putting her arms around his shoulders and playing with the long ends of his straight brown hair. He really needed a haircut she thought—and then she stopped herself. He was perfect as he was, and she didn't want to remake him.

"Greedy woman, fishing for compliments?" he teased.

"Why not?"

Throwing his head back, he laughed. She joined in. He tweaked her nose. "I don't know if I can put it into words, all I know is that I light up when you come into a room. That I can't get enough of watching you sweep back your gorgeous, unruly red hair. Or enough of the way you walk with your hips swaying and your perfect ass—"

"Manny!"

He grinned. "I thought you wanted to know."

"Sounds more like lust to me, especially the part about my perfect ass."

He rubbed his face with his hand and grinned. "I fell in love with your ass—that first day, when you were bent over your filing cabinet, looking for something."

"Fell in love with my ass—what a thing to say."

"But it's true." He grinned again and kissed the tip of her nose. "When I got to know you better, I found I liked talking to you, being with you." He shook his head and one side of his mouth quirked up. "Even when we argue. It doesn't matter. When I'm around you, I feel content and happy." He ran his hand across her breasts, caressing them. "I will admit there's nothing nicer than this, though."

"Not even hanging wallpaper?"

He laughed again. "Not even that."

They kissed and drew apart.

"Now...about that wall I wanted to put in," he said.

"Oh, Manny, I can't thank you enough for stopping me from falling."

"Forget it." He tucked in his lips and shook his head.

She glanced around. "I'm worried a wall will make this room seem so small."

"What about a half-wall?" His eyes gleamed and he cupped one breast, lifting it to his mouth. A shudder of pure pleasure pulsed through her.

"You can't say you don't need privacy now."

No, she couldn't say that. Her mind spun, turning cartwheels. What did he mean? That he would stay with her and love her, and they'd need privacy. Or was she grasping at straws—wanting his words to mean more than they did?

He lowered his mouth again and suckled her, and his hands strayed lower, playing with the swollen wet folds of her and circling her clit with his fingers.

She clung to him, giving herself over to the pleasure, not wanting to think any more, not wanting to worry about losing him. He was hers for now—and that was all that mattered.

At least, that's what she told herself.

***

Manny stretched his long legs beneath the cramped table. The loud music pulsed and throbbed. Dancers spun by. Grabbing his Lone Star beer, he took a sip but his gaze never left Catalina. It wasn't easy to keep track with her dancing in the arms of a stranger in the dark honky-tonk.

They'd crammed a year's worth of living into the past few weeks. He'd finished her bedroom, complete with a sturdy half-wall where the railing had been. But he'd taken lots of breaks, and they'd indulged themselves in bed until they were both sore in unmentionable places.

Grinning to himself, he hadn't known he had it in him, especially at his age, and especially after his self-imposed celibacy. But with Cat as his willing bed partner, he was like a horny teenager. No matter how much they made love, he couldn't get enough of her.

She'd put away Nieto's picture. He hadn't asked her to, but one day he'd noticed the picture was gone. He'd started to say something and stopped. What she did with her late husband's picture wasn't his business. Given how their marriage had ended, he'd wondered why she kept the painful reminder in her bedroom. Probably to honor the good years of their marriage. He couldn't fault her for wanting to keep those memories.

Catalina swept by, her hips swaying to the salsa beat. The guy who'd asked her to dance had to be about fifteen years younger. But you couldn't tell by looking at Catalina. Dressed in a tight green sheath, she'd already turned a lot of heads tonight.

Manny had danced with her until his feet hurt and his legs felt stiff. He didn't know where she got the energy or stamina. He was in pretty good shape, but on the dance floor he had trouble keeping up with her frenetic pace.

She did everything with passionate abandon. Since they'd started dating, she'd taken him everywhere: to dinner, to movies, and dancing. He enjoyed their outings but not as much as their quiet evenings when they stayed home and one of them cooked and they made slow, sensual love. The night he'd given her a bubble bath and massage had been one of his particular favorites.

They'd even double dated a couple of times with Esme and Hank. But the last time they'd been out with the couple, Manny had noticed his neighbor and girlfriend didn't appear as happy as they had in the beginning. He hoped their relationship wasn't coming apart, just as he and Cat were growing closer. He'd meant to stop by Hank's trailer and see how he was doing, but he found himself spending every possible moment with Catalina.

Taking another sip of his beer, he realized the loud music had ended. Couples on the dance floor drifted apart. Flushed and laughing, Catalina grabbed his hands, urging him back on the floor.

He groaned but got to his feet. A slow love song came on, and he was grateful for the respite and eager for the chance to hold her in his arms. Enfolding her in his embrace, they swayed to the music. He smelled the vanilla in her hair, savored her lush curves pressed against his too-willing body. And wished this night would never end.

But that was the problem—it was going to end too soon.

Already the days had grown longer and warmer. His kids had called several times, wondering why he hadn't come home. One time, they'd all managed to get together at Rita's house and talked to him on Skype. He'd made excuses, but he hadn't told them about Cat.

What was he going to do? How could he leave her? But he couldn't stay, and she'd never consent to come with him. Would she?

He was in love with her, and he didn't know what to do about it.

***

Catalina sat on a campstool, sipping lemonade, watching Manny's big hands fashion a lump of driftwood into a piece of art. His deft movements fascinated her, how he could coax an image from an unyielding chunk of wood.

But everything about Manny fascinated her. His big, callused hands, so gentle when he touched her. The way he laughed and the deep rumble of his voice. How he danced, as if putting his heart and soul into the music. His impassioned attempts at cooking. How he got teary-eyed at nostalgic movies. She'd never known a man who cried at movies. And the way he made love, slow and sensual, giving her bubble baths and massages, lighting candles and incense. Nibbling strawberries with her in bed.

He was a man of many parts, as they said in classic novels. And she never tired of learning new facets of him.

So sweet and giving and thoughtful—her Manny.

She'd loved her husband dearly until that last year of their marriage. She'd never thought to find another to replace him. But God had been good, giving her Manny when she'd believed she would spend the rest of her life alone.

He glanced up and smiled. She returned his smile. He wiped the perspiration from his forehead with his arm. The simple gesture jolted her, bringing her back to reality.

The days were getting hotter.

He'd already stayed longer than three months. She'd overheard some of his conversations with his kids, and she knew they were eager for him to return, especially his daughter who was having a baby.

Thinking about him leaving, her stomach heaved and she felt nauseous. How could she let him go? How could he leave her? Nothing had been said about their relationship. She'd put away her late husband's picture, hoping Manny would say something about their future. But he hadn't commented.

Dios, she prayed, closing her eyes and begging, *don't give him to me, only to take him away.*

Why hadn't Manny said anything? Not even that he loved her. She loved him with all her heart. A hundred times, she'd had to choke back the words. But she wouldn't throw herself at him. It wasn't right. He was the man—he should say something first.

How could he not love her when they'd shared the most intimate lovemaking she'd ever experienced? When their souls and hearts touched each time they made love? Or for him, was their lovemaking just about sex, as she'd feared in the beginning? Could he walk away and leave her without a moment's regret?

Fear sliced through her. She couldn't stay still, thinking about his leaving. Worrying he didn't love her. She got to her feet and grabbed his empty glass. "I'll get you some more lemonade. Okay?"

"*Gracias, mi amorcita*," he replied without looking up.

"*Mi amorcita*," my love. He'd called her that since they'd made love that first afternoon in her bedroom. But him calling her his love wasn't enough, not nearly enough. She wanted him to *declare* his love.

And she prayed if he did love her, he would want to marry her, and they would spend the rest of their lives together. She'd never wanted anything so much in her life—not even the Park.

***

Catalina lay sprawled naked on the bed while Manny massaged her shoulders and back. His hands strayed to her buttocks, cupping and fondling them. She wriggled on the bed, savoring their slow, sensual foreplay. Knowing before he was through, she'd be begging for her release.

Thinking about their lovemaking filled her with a tingling kind of anticipation, as if her entire body was one raw, sensitive nerve, jangling with erotic awareness.

The phone shrilled beside the bed.

Manny's hands stilled. "Don't answer it," he said. "Whoever it is will call back."

She almost agreed but then she remembered it was Sunday. Her children always called on Sundays. "I think it might be Carlos or Alba."

"Oh, all right." He sounded disappointed and moved to the other side of the bed.

She grabbed the receiver. "*Bueno*."

"*Mamá*, hello, how are you doing?"

Sitting up, she drew the chenille bedspread over her body, almost as if her son could see her nakedness over the phone. "Carlos, I'd hoped you would call. How are you and Alba?"

"We're both fine. She said she'd call later."

"That's good. Work going okay?"

"Yes, work is great."

"That's good." She was mouthing the usual polite words. Was her preoccupation with Manny making her distant with her children? She didn't want to go there again, to repeat the past when she'd forgotten what was important.

But Manny was important, too, wasn't he? Or was he? Would he be walking out of her life, and she'd be starting over again—with only her children?

"Elena called me," he said.

She was surprised. "Why on earth would she do that?"

"She's worried about you, *Mamá*. She told me the taxes on the Park doubled and you were having trouble with the County inspector."

Catalina was surprised Elena had alerted her son. Her best friend knew things were starting to turn around. She wondered what had prompted Elena's phone call—and then she knew. Her friend had called several times during the past few weeks to chat, but Catalina had cut her short, being caught up with Manny. And because she wasn't sure where their relationship was headed, she'd purposely avoided talking about it.

"Don't worry, *m'ijo*, that's been settled now." She pushed her free hand through her hair. "I've been busy with the Park and haven't talked to Elena."

From the corner of her eye, she saw Manny scowl. *So it was a white lie.* Did he want her to tell her son they stayed in bed so much, she'd neglected her best friend?

"Oh, I guess that explains why she was worried. You should call Elena."

"I will as soon as we get off. Okay?"

"Yeah, that's good. But Elena said you had to go to a hearing on the taxes to get them to come down."

"That's true."

"Then the Park is doing better financially?"

"Yes, everything is under control. I got the Park repairs done and had enough left over to remodel my home."

"Really, I'm surprised. And I don't know if I believe you. Since what happened at Christmas, you don't always tell me the whole truth."

"You're starting to sound lIke *my* parent." She glanced at Manny. He made a face, as if he understood grown kids acting like that.

"*Mamá*, I worry about you. Have the developers been back?" Carlos sucked in his breath. "Damn it! I wish you'd take their offer."

She sighed and thought about chastising him for cursing. Given her past record in that department, she held her tongue. "The developers haven't been back. And I don't want their money. I'm not selling."

Manny shook his head and looked away. She wondered what that meant.

"Okay, okay. But how can you pay the raise in taxes, not to mention all the remodeling you've done?"

"I got a loan from the bank."

"But I thought you didn't want to be in debt."

"I don't," she said. "It's only temporary, though. The Park is full and doing really well. You should see the place; you wouldn't recognize it." She grabbed Manny's hand and squeezed it. "I couldn't have done it without a certain contractor who saved my life."

Glancing at Manny, she smiled. He didn't return her smile, and he let go of her hand. He rose from bed and started putting on his clothes.

What was wrong with him?

"What's this about a contractor?" Carlos asked.

She wondered what else Elena might have told her son. She'd discussed Manny with Elena, and she knew her friend didn't approve of her getting involved with a snowbird.

She took a deep breath. "His name is Manuel Batista, and he's been staying at the Park. He's a carpenter and he's worked wonders, *mi hijo*. I wasn't kidding when I said you should see the Park now. And he renovated my house, too. It looks like home beautiful."

Fully dressed, Manny leaned down and gave her a quick kiss on the cheek. She grabbed for his hand, wanting him to stay. He frowned and turned away. She felt desperate being trapped on the phone. She wanted to ask where he was going, but she didn't want to alert Carlos.

"I'm happy the Park and your house are fixed up. Sounds great. Tell me more about this Manuel. Where is he from? You say he's a carpenter? But he's just a snowbird. Right?"

So Elena had talked to her son about Manny. She wanted to answer her son's questions, but she couldn't get her mind off Manny. He'd left her bedroom and descended the stairs. Where was he going? Had her son's call disturbed him? Had Manny wanted her to explain their relationship and not categorize him as her carpenter?

But what *was* their relationship? Nothing had been settled. Even her son knew he was a snowbird and assumed he'd be leaving. Thinking about it, her heart wrenched.

"*Mamá?*" Carlos prompted.

"*Hijo*, I'll call you later and explain everything. But don't worry. I'm fine and the Park is doing well." She paused. "I'm sorry I didn't tell you before, but I didn't want to burden you or make you feel like you had to help. I want you to concentrate on your career."

"You mean you didn't want to hear me curse the Park and all its problems."

Why couldn't he let well enough alone? She didn't want to get angry and argue. She wanted to go to Manny.

"Probably you're right, Carlos. Guilty as accused. But the crisis is past."

"I still want to know about this Manuel and—"

"*Hijo*," she made her voice stern, "I'll call you later. Okay? *Adios*." And then she hung up the phone and pulled on her clothes.

Chapter Eleven

Manny closed and locked his trailer door. He hadn't realized how late it was because he'd slept most of the day. He wanted to take Catalina to dinner and break the news. He'd made up his mind. No more drifting.

He had to tell Cat he'd be leaving within the week. She'd come to him after talking to her son, and they'd made love all night. He'd meant to tell her then, but he couldn't bring himself to do it.

Her son's call had made Manny stop and think. If he and Catalina continued, her children would find out. Better to leave before other people were involved and expectations were raised. He didn't want Catalina to be put in the position of explaining to her children about their relationship.

He cared deeply for her. And if he wasn't painfully aware of the choices and distances keeping them apart, he would have admitted his love and asked her to marry him.

But if he did ask her—where would they live? His entire family was in Chicago. Cat wasn't as close to her children because they lived in Houston. He could ask her to move to Chicago except for one thing—the Park. He knew how important it was, and hearing her defend the place to her son yesterday had driven the point home.

They were at an impossible impasse.

But he didn't want to give her up. He planned to write and call and fly down during the year. He still wanted a relationship, a *monogamous* relationship. And he'd return next winter. Maybe the situation would resolve itself and one of them could see their way clear to uproot their lives. In the meantime, he didn't want to talk of love—to lead her on. That seemed cruel.

A silver Prius was parked in her driveway. He'd never seen the car before; no one in the Park drove a Prius. And the Park was full. He wondered whose car it was. Maybe the developers had returned.

He pushed open the front door and walked into the reception area. As usual, the room was deserted, which was odd because he'd expected to see the owner of the Prius. He heard voices coming from the back and relaxed a fraction. The car must belong to a friend. He decided not to intrude. He turned around and pulled open the door. The bell jangled.

Damned jangling bell.

"Manny." Catalina's voice stopped him.

He really didn't feel like meeting Cat's friends and making small talk, especially considering what he wanted to discuss. But he couldn't slink away now.

With a smile in place, he faced her. "I thought you had company, and I didn't want to intrude."

She returned his smile. "I do have company, but I want you to meet them. My kids popped in, surprising me. I guess they were worried about their mother."

Manny groaned inwardly. Just the kind of meeting he'd been dreading. Would her kids guess at their relationship and resent him? The possibilities for a less-than-pleasant confrontation boggled his mind.

A young man and woman joined Catalina. It wasn't hard to see they were her kids, especially the son. Neither of them had her red hair; their hair was dark brown, and the girl was taller and thinner than Cat.

Catalina's daughter looked almost ethereal, with huge green eyes. The boy had brown eyes but his mouth and the shape of his face were definitely Catalina's.

"Manny Batista, I'd like you to meet Carlos and Alba, my son and daughter," she said.

Alba nodded and gave him a shy smile. Carlos crossed the room with his hand extended. Manny shook his hand. "Pleased to meet you." He nodded in Alba's direction. "Your mother talks a lot about both of you. I feel as if I know you already."

"And we're glad to meet you, too," her son said. "*Mamá* showed us around. You've done a remarkable job with the Park and her home. Everything looks new and updated."

Catalina caught his eye and smiled again. He wished he shared her joy at this "surprise" visit. Didn't she realize her kids hadn't taken a day off from work without a powerful reason?

And he knew the reason—they wanted to inspect him.

As a matter of fact, Alba was doing just that. She'd narrowed her eyes and was looking him up and down. Carlos was busy raving about the renovations, but Manny knew the young man was sizing him up, too.

"*Gracias*, Carlos, I'm happy you're pleased with the repairs. The Park almost runs itself now," he added for Catalina's benefit, knowing she and her son didn't agree on keeping the property.

"I'm glad, really glad. *Mamá* explained about the County inspector and his ridiculous deadlines. If it hadn't been for you—"

"Your mother would have found someone else. I'm sure the County would have given her an extension if necessary."

"You're awfully modest, aren't you, Mr. Batista?" Alba chimed in, opening her mouth for the first time. "The Park looks wonderful. And *Mamá* tells me you're an artist too. I saw the sculpture you gave her. It's beautiful. I'm also an artist or at least...I try."

"I didn't know that," he said, "though your mother mentioned you were in design. What do you do?"

"Mostly paint." Laughing, she tilted her head, reminding him of Catalina. "Unfortunately, unless you're famous, painting doesn't pay the bills." Her comment was obviously meant to convey a subtle reproach, and she gazed at him with an assessing look in her green eyes.

"Uh, you're right about that," Manny agreed. "That's why I'm a carpenter first."

"That's nice," Alba responded, brightening. "You've done a wonderful job around here."

Manny didn't reply. They were starting to repeat themselves. Carlos stood with his hands behind his back, whistling under his breath and rocking back and forth on the balls of his feet.

"It was nice to have met you both," Manny said. "I'll just be going—"

"Don't go, Manny," Catalina said. "Stay to dinner. You can put the steaks on the grill for me."

Two pairs of eyes turned to him, a questioning light in each. He smiled a frozen smile. Didn't Cat realize what she'd said? She'd underscored their domestic relationship. If her kids didn't know before, they certainly knew now.

He realized it was silly of him, worrying about what they thought. Times might have changed, but he and Cat were old-fashioned. And it wasn't any of her kids' business either. Cat might not care if her kids knew, but he did. With their knowledge, he felt as if he was on display—like a strange specimen to be studied—their mother's lover.

"I'll be glad to put the steaks on for you." There was no way he could refuse; he was trapped for the evening.

Despite her children's curiosity, the dinner went well. They talked about Manny's family in Chicago and his sculptures. Carlos discussed his analyst job at an oil and gas firm. Alba blushed when Catalina brought up her daughter's new boyfriend. Then she got very quiet.

In true maternal fashion, Cat poked and prodded about Alba's job. Obviously, her daughter had had trouble finding a job she liked. Manny felt sorry for the girl, and he made a point to try and talk about her painting.

At Manny's urging, Alba finally opened up and prattled on about post-modernism and neo-impressionistic works. Manny listened and nodded, not understanding half of what she was saying.

After dinner while they were enjoying coffee and pound cake, Carlos said, "*Mamá* explained why you put a half-wall upstairs." He inclined his head toward the bedroom. "We owe you a debt of gratitude for saving her."

Manny blushed. He couldn't help it. Remembering what had happened—in vivid detail—after he'd pulled Cat from the edge made him uncomfortable.

Carlos cleared his throat, sounding as if Manny's embarrassment was catching.

"I, ah, I, that is…" Manny stammered.

Reaching across the table, Cat covered his hand with hers. "Manny's just being modest again. He's a very humble man. But he did save my life."

He shrugged and tried to grin.

Alba and Carlos gazed at him.

He freed his hand and sat back. "I wish there was a bathroom up there," he said, desperate to say something to diffuse the situation. "It would be more convenient than running up and down the stairs, especially at night. Your mother wanted me to replace the railing, but I worried that even with new railing, if she took a wrong step, she might—"

"*Mamá* doesn't need to live like this, you know." Carlos shot his mother a pointed look. "She could sell this place and live like a queen." He stabbed his index finger into the air. "Did you know some developers offered her two million dollars for the property? But she turned them down." His voice was filled with rancor. "I can't talk sense to her."

Manny choked back a gasp. He hadn't realized. He'd known the property was valuable—but two million dollars? Now he understood why her taxes had doubled and why the County expected her to keep up the place. Why hadn't she taken the offer? The Park might be her dream, but common sense should prevail.

"Why so much?" he asked.

"Because most of the properties overlooking the public beach were gobbled up by big corporations as soon as the old Spanish land grant titles were cleared up," Catalina explained. "This Park is one of the few large plots that hasn't been developed.

"And I promised Yolanda to keep the place undeveloped," she added. "To keep the land the way her ancestors found it." She stared at her son. "You wouldn't want a mother who goes back on her word and takes advantage of an old woman. Would you?"

"*Mamá*, you know Yolanda gave you an out—that if you couldn't make the Park work, you could sell. She just didn't want you developing it." He shrugged. "At least that's what you told us when Yolanda's will was read. And now, after what happened at Christmas—"

"Carlos, don't be ridiculous. I'm not in any danger."

"What happened at Christmas?" Manny asked.

"*Mamá* was held up, at gunpoint. The guys wore ski masks and the police haven't caught them yet."

Manny stared at Catalina, a silent accusation in his eyes.

She pushed her hair off her forehead. "It was a couple of kids needing money for Christmas, no doubt. They didn't get much. I'd gone to the bank a couple of days before. And a lot of people pay with plastic."

Manny sucked in his breath. Why hadn't she told him? Because he would worry about her? She would have been right—he was stunned. Call him naïve, but he'd never considered the danger of running a place like this. To contemplate someone robbing her at gunpoint was deeply disturbing. Now he could see why her kids were so concerned.

"I have to agree with Carlos and Alba," Manny said. "It doesn't matter how little money the thugs took. It's what could have happened, especially with guns involved. People have died for a few dollars—it happens all the time at convenience stores."

Alba snapped her fingers. "Listen to Manny. He's talking sense, *Mamá*."

Cat turned in her seat and glared at him. He folded his arms and stared back.

"What would I do with myself if I sold the Park? I'm too young to retire. I've worked hard all my life. I don't think I could spend my days playing bingo and going to dances." She threw up her hands. "I would go nuts within a month."

Stubborn woman. Didn't she see she was throwing away happiness with both hands? Hell, if she sold, they'd have more than enough to buy a condo in the new development. Or he could buy them a condo, and they could spend part of the year here. She could give the money to her kids if she wanted. He'd take care of her, was more than willing to take care of her. They'd marry and spend their time traveling and visiting their families. Why was a promise to an old friend so important, especially if keeping the Park was dangerous?

She could be robbed again. He shook his head.

Alba shook her head, too, and glanced at Carlos and then Manny. "There's no use talking to her—this Park means everything to *Mamá*." She frowned. "Carlos, you should know that—after what happened to our family."

Cat grabbed her daughter's arm. "How can you say that? Did I ever miss one thing at your school? Or your birthdays or ballet recitals or—"

"No, *Mamá*, you were there for all our important events." She shook off her mother's hand. "But you weren't there for *Papá*, were you?"

Cat jerked back as if she'd been slapped. "Alba, this isn't the time or place to talk about our family." She slanted a glance at Manny.

Alba rose from the table. "Why not? Haven't you told your new boyfriend what happened? How you deserted *Papá*, and he got sick and—"

"Alba, that's not how it happened, and you know it. And your father wasn't exactly perfect." Cat stood and glared at her daughter.

The two women faced each other over the table like hissing cats.

Carlos touched Manny's arm. "Let's go outside. Okay?"

Not knowing what to do about Cat and her daughter, he was grateful for the interruption. Pushing to his feet, he said, "Excuse me."

Manny trailed after Carlos. Once outside, the young man stopped next to the silver Prius and leaned against the car with his arms folded

"Nice car," Manny said. "Is it yours?"

"It's not Alba's, I can tell you that." Carlos shook his head. "My sister drives an old VW, a clunker. She spends all her money on canvas and paints. In her own way, she's as much of a dreamer as our mother, but you see how they get along. Like oil and water."

"Mothers and daughters," Manny said.

But it was more than that. Carlos had obviously forgiven his mother for what had happened to his parents' marriage. He was living in the present, wanting his mother to sell the Park for legitimate reasons.

"Yeah, I guess you'd know about that with the size of your family, two daughters and all." Carlos glanced at him. "Do you like the Valley?"

Manny wondered why Carlos had abruptly changed the subject. "I like the Valley. I have relatives in Matamoros."

Carlos smiled and unfolded his arms. "That's great, because I was wondering if you'd consider staying. Not just for the winter but—"

"Wait a minute." Manny held up his hand. "You know I've got four kids and two grandchildren up north, with another grandchild on the way."

"Yeah, but you're retired, right?"

"Semi-retired. Pablo, my oldest wants me retired, but I haven't given up yet." He paused, not knowing how Carlos would react. "I can tell you one thing, and I hope it will put your mind to rest. I'll call the best security company tomorrow and have a state-of-the-art system put in before I leave. My cost, and gift to your mother."

Carlos half-turned and looked him up and down again. "I thought you were a carpenter."

"I was...or I'm still a carpenter, but I own a construction company in Chicago. Pablo is running it for me while I take some time off." He rubbed his jaw. "I was supposed to 'find' myself on this trip and figure out what I wanted to do when I retired."

"So, you have bucks?"

"Pardon me, young man?"

"I guess I'm the one who should be asking your pardon. I thought you needed money—that's why you did the renovation work."

"I did the work for your mother because she needed it done, and the original guy she hired wasn't going to meet the County deadline."

Carlos loosed a low whistle. "So it's more than dating—you're involved with my mother. And you have money, too, owning a construction company and all."

"I'm not fabulously wealthy, but I have money." He hesitated, wanting to tell Carlos how much he cared for Catalina. But somehow, telling her son before he told her didn't seem right.

"And, yes, I care a lot about your mother." He lowered his head. "It's going to be hard to leave—but my children especially my oldest girl, who's expecting, wants me home. I'll make certain your mother is safe before I go."

"I wanted to get her a gun, but she told me she'd probably accidentally shoot herself," Carlos said.

Manny half-smiled. "I think a security system is a better choice, all things considered." He had a sudden thought. "Where was *Migo* when she was held up?"

"Penned outside. Now she keeps him in the house at least." Carlos spread his hands. "But you know how that is—a dog is great for alerting you, but if someone has a gun—"

"They'll shoot the dog." Manny nodded. "I didn't know about the robbery until tonight. If that didn't scare her, I don't know what will. And she knows how you and Alba feel." He shrugged again. "A monitored security system is all I know to do. If she'll let me give it to her," he said to himself, half under his breath.

But Carlos had heard him. "She better let you, or Alba and I will figure out a way to come up with the money."

"Remember your mother is a grown woman, and she's going to do what she wants to do. None of us can make her do what she doesn't want to."

"Yeah, I understand, but it's kind of selfish of her to make us worry."

Manny put his hand on Carlos' shoulder. "Don't worry, I'll convince her about the security system and take care of it." He gazed at Carlos, realizing Catalina's children cared a lot about their mother.

"When you say monitored, you mean—"

"Closed-circuit cameras and feed to the local authorities." He grinned. "And enough alarms to wake up the dead."

"What about the perimeter fence?"

"Sensors on the outside that won't bother the renters but will discourage trespassers."

"Wow, you really know your business."

Manny sighed. "I try to. And I won't leave until it's all set up."

Carlos nodded. "I can't thank you enough. But I believe Alba and I should pay you back." He hesitated. "You and *Mamá* might be close, but it's our responsibility to—"

"I want to do this for your mother." *And a whole lot more.* "Why don't you let me worry about securing the Park?" He squeezed Carlos' shoulder. "And I might be able to convince her to sell, too."

"How are you going to do that?"

Catalina and the Winter Texan

He grinned. "I have a plan."

"I don't see how you can convince her when she won't listen to me."

"Let me try." He released Carlos' shoulder. "You have to get back to work, don't you?"

"Alba and I are driving back tonight."

"I'll talk to your mother and let you know what happens."

"Okay." Carlos pulled out his wallet and retrieved a business card. "That's my work number and cell."

"Great. I'll let you know."

"Sure," Carlos replied, but Manny detected an undertone of doubt in his voice. "I hope you know what you're doing."

Catalina and Alba came out, their arms wrapped around each other.

Manny gazed at them, hoping they'd put the past to bed. If they had, maybe it would make his plan easier. All he could do was try. If she cared about him enough, he could convince her. If not…

He turned to Carlos. "Either way, whether she agrees to sell or not, I promise to call you within the next couple of days." He pulled out his wallet and found his business card. He handed it to Carlos and pointed to the bottom line. "That's my cell. You can reach me any time."

Cat called to him, "Manny, we need to make our goodbyes. Carlos and Alba have to get back to Houston. They have work tomorrow."

Carlos grabbed his hand and pumped it. "Thank you for everything—the security system and trying to get her to sell. You don't know how much this means to me and Alba."

Not as much as it means to me.

***

With Manny by her side and his arm encircling her waist, Catalina waved goodbye to her kids. She didn't know what he'd said to Carlos, but he must have charmed him completely. And Alba had approved of Manny, too.

But what difference did it make—if they didn't have a future together?

Grabbing her hands, Manny said, "Let's go back inside. I need to talk to you."

Catalina caught her breath, anticipating and dreading what might be coming. Her heart thumped painfully in her chest, praying her children's visit had galvanized Manny into action.

Inside he pulled her down on the couch and kissed her thoroughly. When he lifted his head, he said, "I've wanted to do that all night. I thought they'd never leave."

She giggled and ran one finger down the side of his face, resting it against his lips. "Don't say that. They really like you. I couldn't be happier." She smiled.

Gently, he removed her finger. "Cat, I like your kids too. You should be very proud of them." He hesitated. "And I was glad to see you and Alba made up. Am I right?" He hesitated again. "Or if you don't think it's my business, I understand."

"Alba has a quick temper and—"

"Like someone we know." There was a gleam of mischief in his eyes.

"*Sí*, guilty as accused. Sometimes she's too much like me." She smiled. "But like me, she's quick to forgive."

"Really?"

"Oh, we're not there yet, but she'll come around. She was her father's little girl. They were close." This time she was the one who hesitated. "But tonight we finally had a good talk. She's nervous about her new boyfriend because her old one cheated on her and said it was because she spent too much of her free time, painting." She gazed at Manny. "For the first time, she can relate to what I went through. So, I'm hopeful."

"That's good. I'm glad. You and Alba need to put the past behind you."

"I agree, and we're working on it." She tilted her head. "What did you and Carlos talk about?"

"Your safety at the Park."

"Oh, Manny, don't tell me you're going to gang up on me with my son."

He squeezed her hands. "I'm not ganging up on you, but I want you to be safe. If you're here all alone, you need a security system."

Her heart sank. A security system? Really? That's what he was proposing? A bunch of metal and wires?

She pulled her hands free. "Manny, I can't afford a security system, you know that."

"Yes, but I can. Let me give you a security system. I want you to be safe."

So that was it, payment for services rendered. They'd had an affair, he was leaving, but he wanted to give her a parting gift. Suddenly she felt dirty all over.

And she should have known. A leopard didn't change his spots. He'd been unfaithful to his wife, the mother of his children, for how many years? Just because he'd regretted her death—and thought he'd changed—didn't mean he had.

Why had she forgotten the kind of man he was?

Manny's cell buzzed. He pulled out the phone and looked at the caller ID. "*Lo siento*, I'm sorry," he said. "I need to take this. I'll just be a minute."

"No problem, take your time."

Not wanting to eavesdrop, she rose and crossed to the kitchen. *Migo* came and nudged her leg. She patted her dog's head. Then she opened the refrigerator and tried to concentrate on what she'd make tomorrow night for dinner. Despite her best intentions, she couldn't help but overhear Manny's one-sided conversation.

"Rita, I'm glad you called," he said. "How are you doing?"

There was a pause.

"The doctor said that?" he asked.

Manny listened for a long time.

"I'll be home by the first of next week, *mi niña*, you can count on me."

Catalina didn't want to hear any more. He was leaving and going home. His pregnant daughter needed him. She could understand and sympathize, but she needed him too.

Today had been a long day, a veritable roller coaster of emotions. Despite the brave face she'd put on for Manny, she'd been filled with apprehension when her children had shown up. She'd known they would put him through a grueling inspection. And Alba would be resentful of anyone taking her father's place.

But in the end, her children had approved. Now Manny's daughter had called, wanting her father. Catalina felt as if they were embroiled in a tug-of-war with no end in sight.

Feeling as if her heart was being cut from her chest with a blunt instrument, she grabbed her dog's collar. "How about a run on the beach, *Migo*?"

With *Migo* trailing behind, she sprinted down the path to the beach. Once she got there, she stood at the edge of the lapping waves, staring at the black ocean. Overhead, billions of stars spangled the sky. The new moon had already set. *Migo* ran around and around, turning in circles and barking, enjoying the unexpected outing.

Before being held up at gunpoint, she used to walk the beach at night. Not anymore. Shivering, she folded her arms and hugged her waist.

Migo raced down the beach, barking at something. She started to call him back but found her voice was a mere squeak. Her chest felt compressed as if someone was sitting on it, and her throat was raw. Tears seeped from the corners of her eyes. With an angry backhand, she dashed them away.

When she felt hands touch her bare shoulders, she started and almost screamed. She hadn't heard him approach; the sand must have muffled his footsteps. But she knew it was Manny. If she lived to be a thousand years old, she'd never forget the touch of his callused hands.

"Why didn't you tell me about being held up?" he asked.

"I didn't think it was important."

Gently, he turned her around until she faced him. "It's important because you were in danger."

She shrugged free and backed up a pace. "Why do you act like you care, Manny? You're leaving, going home. I heard you talking." She bit her lip. "I wasn't trying to listen, but the room is—"

"You don't have to explain. And I don't care if you hear all of my conversations for the rest of my life."

She stopped breathing, stopped moving, even her heart seemed to stop beating in her chest. What did he mean?

He grabbed her hand and pulled her to him. "Cat, I do care for you. I don't want to lose you, and I don't want to worry about you being alone and vulnerable. Do you care for me?"

Gazing at him, she stared into his eyes for a long time, hoping this wasn't a dream or a joke or a fantasy playing in her head.

"What do you propose, Manny? You know I care, but you're leaving."

"I know." He gathered her into his arms and held her close. "I want a relationship with you, even if it's long distance. When your kids told me how much you'd been offered to sell the place and that you could be in danger, staying here, but you won't listen to them..." His voice trailed off. "I knew what I suspected was true—you won't give up this place for anything or anyone. But despite that, I want us to be together as much as possible. My family is in Chicago, but I can fly down during the year and spend the winters here." He hesitated. "Eventually, maybe things will work out. Maybe you'll want to—"

"Sell the Park?"

But what was he offering, a long-distance romance, not marriage? Why should she sell the Park for that? And even if he offered marriage, she had no intention of giving up her dream—the dream she'd fought so hard for. The dream she'd given up everything for. Why were his family and commitments more important than hers?

Because he could keep their relationship and have another woman or two in Chicago?

He cupped her chin in his hand. "If you would consider selling, let me take care of you, Cat. Sell this place and give the money to your kids. I don't think you should stay here by yourself, even with a security system. Carlos is right—it's not safe. And the struggle you've been through—is a dream worth it?" He brushed her lips with his. "We'll make our own dreams, Cat."

Make our own dreams—what did he mean? He still hadn't said he loved her only that he "cared." And he hadn't offered marriage, either. What did he want—a live-in girlfriend?

She felt as if there was a spring in her chest, and with every word he uttered, the spring wound tighter and tighter, cutting off the air to her lungs, strangling her, stopping her heart.

She pulled free again. "I don't know what you mean, Manny." She closed her eyes and dropped her head. "And I don't want a long-distance relationship." She took a deep breath. "I don't know if I can trust you...not after what you told me about your marriage and what happened."

He gasped. "After everything we've been to each other, you don't trust me?"

She shook her head.

And why *should* she trust him? If he hadn't told her he loved her or wanted to stay or wanted to marry her...then she was nothing more than one of his girlfriends.

Migo returned and circled her with a stick in his mouth. "Not now, *Migo*. Sit, boy and stay." Obedient, the Lab dropped the stick and sat back on his haunches.

She folded her arms over her chest. "No, I don't trust you, Manny. And I don't want to be your long-distance girlfriend, worrying who you're with in Chicago and what you're doing." She shook her head. "I trusted before, my husband of twenty-plus years and look where it got me—"

"I was honest with you. I bared my heart and told you how I'd changed." He clenched his hand into a fist. "And now you use it against me? I can't believe you—"

"Believe it."

He curled his lip. "Okay, Catalina, blame me. I'm the bad guy, not you. Never you, you're perfect. Despite what your kids might think. Right?" He flung out his arm. "But I don't think I'm the problem—the real problem is this place. Your Park. You don't want anything to take away from this place, not your former husband or your kids...or me." He dropped his arm and opened his hand. "You're afraid if we stay involved, you might want to sell this place and find a new life with—"

"Don't flatter yourself."

He frowned and shook his head. "Okay, I got it. I can't reason with you. You might not believe me, but I would have been faithful. I would have sworn any oath you wanted. But that's not what you want. You don't want a man; you want a handyman to take care of your property." He spat on the ground. "Have your damned Park and welcome to it. And I hope it keeps you warm on cold nights." Manny turned his back on her and strode down the beach.

Migo barked and got to his feet. The Lab jumped up and placed his paws on her chest, licking her chin and whining for attention.

She stroked her dog's soft fur, trying to soothe her pet. She guessed *Migo* could sense her anguish and was trying to comfort her. But it wasn't enough. Not nearly enough.

Chapter Twelve

Catalina stumbled up the bluff with *Migo* at her heels. Tears poured from her eyes, streaming down her face. Her chest heaved with the effort, and she wiped at her eyes.

When she got inside, she closed and locked the front door. Who was she locking out? Not Manny. He was gone for good. She went to the kitchen and grabbed a paper towel, blowing her nose and wiping her eyes.

Taking a deep breath, she decided to shower and go to bed. The routine would calm her. But when she stood on the first step of the stairs, she knew she couldn't go up there. The sheets smelled of Manny, and heaven help her but she didn't have the strength to change them.

Her home was empty and alien. If she listened carefully enough, she could hear the echo of Manny's voice. Covering her ears with her hands, she tried to turn off her tortured thoughts. Was she going crazy?

She might be crazy, but she knew one thing. She couldn't stay here, not feeling like this. She needed someone to talk to, a shoulder to cry on. Her kids were on their way to Houston. Now, when she glanced at her wristwatch, she saw it was after eleven. The time didn't matter. She'd go to Elena. Her best friend would listen and comfort her.

She grabbed her purse and car keys and headed toward her old neighborhood. When she got there, she pounded on the door but worried Elena and her husband were asleep.

When Elena opened the door, dressed in a woolly, quilted robe with her short brown hair done in pink rollers, Catalina fell into her arms.

"What's this, *chica*?" Elena asked.

Enfolded in her best friend's arms, she started crying again. She sniffed and took deep breaths, wanting to stop her tears. She was tired of crying, and self-pity never helped anyone.

"I'm sorry if I woke you," she said. "I hope I didn't disturb Alberto."

"I wasn't asleep. You know I'm a night owl." Elena snorted. "As for Alberto, he could sleep through a freight train in our bedroom."

Catalina nodded, thankful she hadn't woken Elena or her husband. Thinking about a freight train in her friend's bedroom gave her the giggles, though. She covered her mouth with her hand, but she couldn't stop laughing.

Was she hysterical—crying one minute and laughing the next?

Her friend eyed her. "Come to the kitchen." Elena inclined her head. "I've got coffee."

Catalina followed, wanting to get her own coffee, but Elena made her sit. She needed to stop hiccupping. She tried holding her breath.

Elena glanced at her, a worried expression on her face. "You haven't been drinking, have you?"

"Of course not." Hiccup. "Would I come to your home drunk?" She tried holding her breath again. This was too embarrassing, and if she weren't so upset it would be funny.

"Here, drink this," Elena said, giving her a glass of water. "I'll get the coffee. And if you're hungry, I have some—"

"Nothing to eat," she groaned. "*Por favor*, I'll be sick. Just coffee."

When Elena joined her, they sipped their coffee in silence for a few moments. Catalina took another sip of water and realized the hiccups were gone. She tried to get a handle on her confused thoughts, but they circled in her head, not making any sense.

"Man trouble?" Elena finally asked.

She nodded.

"Tell me about it."

"You called Carlos and told him about Manny. Didn't you?"

Elena reached across the table and patted her hand. "*Sí*, I was worried about you. You didn't return my calls and—"

"Well, you were right. The kids came because they were worried. But they liked Manny."

Elena nodded. "That's good. But if they liked him, why are you here? What's the problem, *amiga mía*?"

Catalina stared at her best friend for a long time, trying to marshal her unruly thoughts. And then, like a dam bursting, everything came pouring out. About Manny and his marriage and what had happened between him and his wife. And about their affair and Manny's offer of a long-distance relationship.

When she stopped to take a sip of coffee, Elena patted her shoulder. "Is that all?"

"Except that I'm slowly dying inside, inch by inch."

"You don't think he'll come back? That he'll reconsider and offer marriage?"

"I don't know, Elena, but I doubt it." She shook her head. "And even if he did, he will want me to give up the Park and move to Chicago where his family is."

"Is giving up the Park such a bad idea, Catalina? I've watched you sacrifice everything for that property." She shook her head. "You almost lost your children over it, though I'm glad to hear they're coming around." Elena lifted one hand, palm out. "I'm not saying I blame you for what Nieto did. He made his choice. God rest his soul." She crossed herself. "But is the Park all you want? Can you keep living there like a hermit and be happy? Are you certain you're being fair to Manny?" She shrugged. "I don't know the man, and that's part of the reason I wanted your children to meet him. But based on everything you've told me about him, he's good and kind and giving. He's helped you a lot." Elena caught her gaze and held it. "Could he be afraid of rejection? Seeing what you've given up for the Park, he's afraid to ask for more than a long-distance relationship? I'm your best friend, and I'm afraid to come between you and your dream."

"But what about his unfaithfulness to his wife? I can't go through that again. Nieto hurt me too much."

Elena shook her head again. "Only you know whether you can trust him or not." She shrugged. "*Amiga mía*, only you can know. You might give him time and see if he honors your long-distance relationship." She took Catalina's hands and squeezed them. "Based on what you've told me and your children's approval, I wish you would give him a chance." She grimaced. "Getting older is hard. Getting older by yourself is doubly hard. And I want you to be happy. Give happy a chance. For me, if nothing else."

Catalina bowed her head. What Elena said was true. Though her dream of the Park had kept her going—it hadn't taken away her loneliness. As desperately as she'd thrown herself into work, she hadn't gotten over her husband's betrayal and death. Hadn't felt at peace in a long time.

Until the last few weeks.

She loved Manny with all her heart and soul. And he was alive, a living being. The Park was a dead thing, made up of utility poles and concrete slabs. Why had she clung to it for so long? Because when Nieto had deserted her, she didn't have anything else?

"But he hasn't said he loves me or offered marriage, Elena."

"I told you, it might be because he doesn't think he can compete with your attachment to the Park." She placed her hands on Catalina's shoulders. "Don't you see? He might be as afraid of rejection as you are. Try to compromise with him. I don't think he'll make you give up the Park, not after all the help he's given you." Her friend dropped her hands. "Give a little, open yourself to him. I think you'll be pleasantly surprised. And your children—don't forget them. They liked him. Trust their instincts."

Oh, if only her friend was right. She didn't want Manny to leave. Should she bend and give a little, as Elena suggested?

"Okay, I'll try. And I hope you're right."

Elena smiled.

Catalina finished her coffee and rose. "I can't thank you enough for talking with me. And for sending my children too. That was important."

Elena rose and hugged her, chuckling. "I think I should start charging for lovelorn advice."

Catalina stepped back. "What do you mean?"

"Do you know Esmeralda Garcia?"

"*Sí*, Manny and I went on a couple of double dates with her. She's dating another renter of mine, Hank McCall. Hank and Manny are friends."

"Well, she bought a house down the road, a couple of months after you sold your home," Elena said. "And we've become friends."

"Esme and Hank had a great relationship going, but now they've run into problems. She came over this afternoon to talk." Elena grinned. "That's why I said I should charge for lovelorn advice—first Esme and now, you."

Catalina hugged her friend. "*Sí*, maybe you should charge, you're good at it." She released Elena and stepped back. "I hope they work it out, like I'm trying to."

"That's kind, but they have financial concerns, and at our stage in life that's serious business." Elena patted her arm. "But you and Manny don't need to worry about finances. You own a valuable property, and Manny is very wealthy."

Catalina dropped her hands to her hips and frowned. "Oh, and how do you know about Manny's finances?"

"The Internet and our subscription to Dun and Bradstreet. Alberto subscribes to check up on his customers and suppliers." Elena winked. "I took the liberty of looking up Manny's construction business, and it has an A-plus rating. That man is the real thing."

***

When Catalina got back to the Park, she saw Manny's trailer was dark and his pickup was missing. Even more disturbing, he'd unhooked his trailer from the utility pole.

There was no doubt he was leaving.

Then she'd wait up for him. Returning to the A-frame, she stationed herself in the office at the front window so she could watch. And she paced for what seemed like hours. *Migo* joined her, prancing alongside and wagging his tail as if they were playing a game.

When she got tired, she flopped down in a chair and put her feet up. Manny couldn't stay away much longer. Could he? *Migo* sat patiently at her side, and she trailed her fingers over his silky fur.

Her eyelids grew heavy. But she didn't dare fall asleep. Rising, she went to the kitchen and made instant coffee. She returned to the office and sat down, grimacing when she sipped the bitter brew. Instant wasn't like real coffee, but she didn't want to leave the window long enough to make real coffee.

Cupping the hot mug in her hands, she gazed out the window, hoping Manny would return. She forced herself to finish the coffee and set her mug down. The coffee warmed her but didn't banish her drowsiness.

She fell asleep with her hand resting on her dog's shoulder.

***

Manny climbed the bluff and walked to his trailer. Out of long habit, he glanced at the A-frame and saw it was dark and Catalina's car was missing from the carport.

That was good, he thought grimly. He didn't want to see her again. Didn't want to face her and have more arguments. What was the use?

He lit two of his hurricane lanterns and proceeded to unhook his utilities in the wavering light. He planned on leaving before sunup.

Swinging into his Ram pickup, he'd decided to gas up and buy a few supplies. The convenience stores were pricey but at least they were open at this time of night. Thirty minutes later, he had a full tank of gas and some groceries. He could leave now. He wasn't going to be able to sleep anyway.

Then he saw the red blinking lights of the honky-tonk. The welcoming glow of the lights beckoned him. He pulled into the sandy parking lot.

Three longnecks later, he didn't feel any better. Only a bit fuzzier and cotton-mouthed. He'd nursed the beers and stewed in his own juices. It was past two o'clock in the morning, and the bar was closing down. In a minute, they'd kick him out.

It didn't matter. He'd stopped at the bar so he wouldn't have to go back to the Park. He'd never been much of a drinker, and he knew better than to think booze might be an answer.

Covering his face with his hands, he thought about what had happened between him and Cat. After Lydia passed away, he hadn't expected to fall in love again. But he'd fallen head over heels for Catalina Reyes, and he knew there was no going back.

Catalina might say she cared for him, but she certainly didn't trust him. And what had really hurt was she'd used his confession against him. He shook his head. But that was just a cover. All she really cared about was her Park. Wasn't it obvious? She didn't want a long-distance relationship because he wouldn't be there to help with the Park.

Which reminded him of his promise to Carlos—that he wouldn't leave until he'd had a state-of-the-art security system installed. But after what Cat and he had said to each other, he couldn't hang around. He could contact a local security company and have the system installed and pay for it, even if he wasn't there to oversee the installation. At least he would keep that part of his promise to Carlos.

All he'd wanted was for them to be together as much as possible within the constraints of their situation. All he'd wanted was to take care of her...and love her. Marry her, if possible. Couldn't Cat understand? Hadn't he worn his heart on his sleeve without actually saying the words?

But what was the use? She didn't trust him and he doubted she really cared. All she cared about was her Park. A piece of land on a beach was more important than their relationship.

***

Catalina woke with a start and untangled herself from the chair. *Migo* lay sleeping at her feet. The first streaks of dawn illuminated the horizon. She heard a car motor outside and then she remembered.

Manny.

She'd been waiting up for Manny. And despite the coffee, she'd fallen asleep. Rushing to the front window, she saw his space was empty.

He was gone!

A hundred curses scorched the early morning. *Migo* woke up and stretched. Seeing how upset she was, he jumped up and put his paws on her shoulders and licked her face. She patted his head and ordered him down. Then she pulled open the front door.

Not knowing what she was doing or where she was going, she ran down the driveway. Like a mirage wavering in the distance, she thought she glimpsed a flash of silver. It was his silver Airstream—she knew it. The sound of the motor must have been Manny leaving the Park.

She'd missed him by seconds.

Her mind spun, grasping at straws. She could follow him. She pivoted and sprinted for the carport. Then she stopped.

It was too late. She might catch up because he was pulling a trailer. But then what? Get him to pull over so she could throw herself at his feet? What if he didn't want to pull over? What if he ignored her and told her to go home?

He'd obviously taken pains to avoid her. He hadn't come home until late last night, and he'd left before first light. He didn't want to see her. Maybe his leaving was for the best.

She bit her lip and fisted her hands, digging her fingernails into her palms. Tell her heart that—*his leaving was for the best*. Doubling over at the waist, she fought the waves of pain rolling over her. The pure, undiluted agony of knowing she'd lost him.

Gulping air, she stood bent over for what seemed like a long time. The edge of the sun peeked above the horizon. Slowly, carefully, she straightened her back. The pain had diminished, settling into a dull, throbbing ache.

Facing home, she started back again and stopped once more. A strange sensation, almost a premonition overtook her. She wanted to stand at the end of the driveway and look for his trailer. But that was silly. He was long gone now.

Her feet didn't obey her logic, and she trudged back to the road. The two lanes were empty. Not even the flash of silver in the distance.

This was ridiculous. She needed to go back and feed *Migo* and let him out to run. Make some coffee and take a shower. Act normal. Take up her life again. She smiled grimly. What life? Her life would never be the same.

She could always call him. She had his cell number. He'd given it to her after the time he'd stayed away in Matamoros.

But what would she say? I'm willing to give up the Park for you. What if he'd changed his mind? What if he didn't want her on *any* terms?

And why was she standing here, gazing at an empty horizon?

***

Manny had never had so much trouble keeping the pickup and trailer on the highway, going in a straight line. The steering wheel wobbled and shuddered in his hands. It was as if the vehicle had a mind of its own and wanted to turn around.

He slammed his hand against the steering wheel. Who was he fooling? Hunks of steel and gears didn't have minds. He was the one who wanted to turn around. Why had he avoided seeing Cat? Maybe he should have gone to her and tried one last time, instead of sneaking away in the night.

Tried what? To convince her to sell the Park and come with him? Was that really fair? He'd lived his dreams, had his family and a successful business. Why was he so quick to snatch *her* dream away? Why had he forced her to make a choice? He'd thought about retiring to the Valley. But when Cat had asked him to stay, he'd refused.

And he'd called her stubborn.

Shaking his head, he wondered if it had been his masculine pride, thinking he knew what was best for her—what was best for them. What if he didn't know what was best? What if they would be happier living here? And over time, she would learn to trust him because he wouldn't stray from her side.

Never stray from her side. Hell, he loved the woman, wanted to marry her.

He could understand her doubts. He'd told her about his past, and it wasn't pretty. And he hadn't committed to her, not really. Hadn't told her he loved her or asked her to marry him. Why? Afraid she'd turn him down? But he'd wanted to see if they could make it, be a couple despite the challenges facing them. Why hadn't he told her last night?

Was he so pathetic that a few angry words had made him give up on the woman he loved? Looking back on their argument, he couldn't believe he'd surrendered so easily, giving in without a fight, abandoning his last chance at happiness.

Hell and damnation!

He yanked the pickup's wheel to the left, almost jackknifing the trailer. When he came to a turnaround, he pulled in and brought the trailer around.

He had to tell her he loved her and wanted to marry her. And if that meant he had to live at the Park; then it was a small sacrifice, considering how happy they would be.

And then he saw her standing at the end of the driveway, looking as if she knew he would be back. His heart took wing and soared. She wanted him as badly as he wanted her. And he couldn't wait—not another second.

He pulled over to the side of the road and jumped out of his cab. He ran to her, his arms stretched wide. Like a shot, she launched herself into his embrace. They hugged and laughed and kissed, dancing along the roadside like two crazy people. Cars whizzed by, and passing motorists threw out catcalls and wolf whistles. But he didn't mind.

He had Catalina in his arms again.

Finally, when they were both gasping for air, they stopped dancing and stood still, swaying in each other's embrace. Manny cradled her face in his hands. Their gazes caught and held.

"You came back," she said.

"You knew I would."

She smiled. "I guess I did." She kissed the back of his hand. "I wanted to go with you."

A shaft of pure joy pierced his heart. She'd changed her mind, was willing to give up everything and move to Chicago. He shook his head. "I don't want you to do that. I want to stay here and help you run the Park."

She pulled back. "Why?" There was a wary look in her eyes.

He went down on one knee, wincing as his knee struck the asphalt. "Because I love you, Cat, and want to marry you. I should have told you sooner, but I guess I didn't want to give you false hopes, not knowing how we'd work things out—where we'd live. Who would have to sacrifice—?"

"Oh, Manny." She reached down and pulled him up. "I love you, too, more than the Park, more than anything." She gulped and gazed at him, tears sparkling on her eyelashes. "And I want to be your wife, no matter where we live. I want...no, *need* to be with you."

"You really mean it? You'd give up the Park...for me?"

She buried her face in his chest. "I would do anything to be with you, Manny. The Park has been wonderful, my dream I worked so hard for." She glanced up at him. "But someone told me it wouldn't keep me warm at night, and he was right, so right." She grinned.

He stroked her hair. "You don't know how happy it makes me to hear you say that. Does that mean you trust me now, too? That you believe I'll be faithful to you for the rest of my—"

"I do, Manny. Deep in my heart, I knew. I was just being stubborn."

"You don't have the corner on stubbornness, *mi amorcita*. I almost let you get away because of my stubbornness."

"Oh, Manny, do you mean that?" She lifted her head again. And this time, he gave in to temptation and kissed her.

He broke their kiss. "Every word, I meant every word."

"What about your family, your kids and grandchildren?"

"That's what airplanes are for."

"But what about Rita and her baby?"

"I need to fly home and be there for the birth. I've promised her."

"You're not going to drive your trailer back?"

"Why would I? I'm here to stay. We need to expand the A-frame and put a master suite downstairs, but I don't mind. It'll keep me busy."

"Are you serious?"

"Perfectly serious. I don't plan on living the rest of my life stumbling down stairs to go to the bathroom."

She laughed. "It's not that bad."

"So you say. But hey, I'm not getting any younger." He grinned. "We'll turn the loft into an extra bedroom for the kids when they come. Maybe we'll put in a screened porch out back for the grandkids. Would you like that?"

"I like everything you do, Manny, especially everything you do in the bedroom."

His cock hardened and grew stiff at her innuendo. Maybe they should continue this discussion inside.

"There's only one thing, Manny, I'd like to get married here on the beach." Grinning, she admitted, "It's a dream of mine."

"Selfish woman." He kissed the tip of her nose. "It will mean a bunch of airplane tickets and getting my brood together. But I'll manage. Will you come with me to see Rita's baby born?"

"But who will run the—"

He scowled and she stopped herself, throwing her arms around his waist and hugging him. "Of course I'll come. After all, Rita's baby will be my first grandchild."

He gazed at her and couldn't help but smile. "That's what I love about you, Cat, your sweet and agreeable nature."

A word about the author

Hebby Roman is the multi-published author of both historical and contemporary romances. Her first contemporary romance, SUMMER DREAMS, was the launch title for Encanto, a print line featuring Latino romances. And her re-published e-book, SUMMER DREAMS, was #1 in Amazon fiction and romance.

Hebby is a member of the Romance Writers of America, and the past president of her local chapter, North Texas Romance Writers. She was selected for the Romantic Times "Texas Author" award, and she won a national Harlequin contest. Her book, BORDER HEAT, was a Los Angeles Times Book Festival selection.

She graduated with highest honors from the University of Texas in Austin with a Master's Degree in Business Administration. She was selected for inclusion in the first edition of Who's Who in American Women.

She is blessed to have all her family living close by in north Texas, including her family's latest edition, her granddaughter, Mackenzie. Hebby lives in Arlington, Texas with her husband, Luis, and maltipoo, Maximillian.

Please visit me at: www.hebbyroman.com or at http://tinyurl.com/q79n4qp.

Thank you

Thank you for reading my book. I hope you enjoyed Catalina and the Winter Texan. Please post your comments or review on my Amazon page at *Hebby Roman*.

Made in the USA
Coppell, TX
03 April 2020